After the Dancing Days

After the Dancing Days

Margaret I. Rostkowski

Harper & Row Publishers, Inc.

To Chuck and David

After the Dancing Days
Copyright © 1986 by Margaret I. Rostkowski
For information address
Harper & Row Junior Books, 10 East 53rd Street,
New York, N.Y. 10022. Published simultaneously in
Canada by Fitzhenry & Whiteside Limited, Toronto.
10 9 8 7 6 5 4 3 2

Library of Congress Cataloging-in-Publication Data
Rostkowski, Margaret I.
    After the dancing days.

    Summary: A forbidden friendship with a badly
disfigured soldier in the aftermath of World War I
forces thirteen-year-old Annie to redefine the word
"hero" and to question conventional ideas of
patriotism.
    [1. World War, 1914–1918—United States—Fiction.
2. Heroes—Fiction.   3. Physically handicapped—
Fiction]   I. Title.
PZ7.R7237Af 1986   [Fic]   85-45810
ISBN 0-06-025077-1
ISBN 0-06-025078-X (lib. bdg.)

Where are your legs that used to run
When first you went to carry a gun?
I fear your dancing days are done.
Johnny, I hardly knew you.

IRISH FOLK SONG

1

My father came home from the war last April. Mother and I drove into town to meet him at the Kansas City train station, the warm day humming around our new Model T as we passed the newly green wheat fields and then the river and then the edges of the city. As we walked to the station, I heard the chug of a train from the tracks hidden below us. What if Father had arrived and we weren't there? After all this time.

I walked, half-running, to the brass doors of the station, pulled them open and stepped into the shadows. Standing a moment to let my eyes adjust, I pulled off my sailor hat and fanned my hot face. Hot for April.

"Annie!" Mother behind me. "You go so fast! I can't keep up with you anymore."

"We've got to be there. I want to be there when . . ."

"I know. I'm anxious to see him too. But we're early." She straightened her wide-brimmed hat and slipped her arm through mine. "Come on. Let's go find him."

We were the first ones at the platform where the troop train was to arrive, except for some men who lounged around two trucks painted with huge red crosses. The men laughed as they leaned across the hoods of the ambulances to exchange cigarettes.

Mother glanced at them and then moved to the very edge of the platform, her hands clenched, the feather on her hat trembling.

A year and a half earlier, my father had left from this

same station. He had explained a little about the war to me, how it had started in 1914 and that Americans were now going to France to fight. I had known all this from school and from the talk around the dinner table for the past three years. And because Uncle Paul had already gone.

"But I'll be stationed in a hospital in New York, Annie. I won't be in any fighting. Not even near. Can you see *me* with a gun?" He chuckled. "So don't worry." He hugged me to him. "Everything will be all right."

I had already seen pen drawings in the newspapers of soldiers with bandaged eyes standing in aid stations, of soldiers lying on hospital beds in France. These were the men my father was now going to help. But even though I knew how much he was needed, I clung to him beside the train the day he left and begged him not to go. I was much younger then.

But now my father was coming home, I was thirteen, and I knew much more about the Great War.

By the time the train was due to arrive, we were surrounded by other wives and children, other families. Mother stood on her tiptoes to see over the crowd, gripping my shoulders for support, looking down the length of the tracks.

I looked at the people around us—women in their bright dresses and big hats, children hiding behind skirts, boys and girls my age in knickers and in middy blouses. Did any of them feel as I did, half elated, half frightened?

I looked down at my hat and tried to smooth out the brim I had crumpled into a mass of wrinkles. Frightened? Not of my father. Life hadn't been the same without him. I had missed him terribly and wanted him home with us. But . . . two years. I had changed.

A cheer. Steam rose above the heads of the crowd as

the train huffed in under the high vault of the station and sighed to a stop.

The healthy men got off first, jumping off the train, running along the platform, searching faces and tumbling into embraces. Handsome, strong men who had gone off like Uncle Paul to fight in the battles we had followed on the maps, to fight because of the kings, the Russian czar and the German kaiser, all the names I had learned in the last two years.

But Uncle Paul would not be coming home, not on this train or any other. One year after he left home for France, he died. As I stood beside my mother on the train platform and watched the men coming home, I thought of the day the telegram came. It was a day in June and I was helping Grandmother make raspberry jam, so I was there to answer the door and to take the telegram from the young boy who stood on the porch and looked sorry. I thanked him and then put the envelope on the hall table.

It had come here. So it wasn't Father. Anyway, he wasn't fighting. He was a doctor. I reached out to the envelope that looked so white against the dark wood, but I didn't touch it.

Who else?

"You know," I told myself. "You know. It has to be him."

As long as I just looked at the envelope, as long as I didn't open it, Uncle Paul was still alive.

"Annie, these berries won't keep. Who's at the door?" Grandmother's voice from the kitchen.

"If I throw away the telegram," I thought, "nothing would change. We could go on, happy . . ."

I reached out to the table, picked up the envelope and turned. Grandfather stood in the door.

I looked at him a moment and then said, "This came,"

3

and I handed him the envelope. And then he knew too, because in 1918 a telegram meant only one thing. Paul was dead.

Now as the soldiers came off the train and ran by me, I looked into each man's face. Maybe it had been a mistake. Maybe Uncle Paul hadn't died after all and was coming home on this train with Father.

The crowd thinned. I took a deep breath and looked at Mother. She put her arm around my shoulder. My hat wouldn't uncurl. Neither would my stomach. I hated waiting.

The platform was now empty except for the few people around us. Still my father did not get off the train.

Suddenly a train door rattled open, far at the end of the platform. A wooden ramp was pushed out and dropped to the pavement below. Mother's hand tightened on my shoulder. A nurse looked out and down the track in our direction. The people around us were silent as the conductor helped the nurse down from the train.

"Mother, where is he?" I whispered, trying to see her eyes under the shadow of her hat.

"He'll be here soon," she answered, her voice unnaturally loud in the now frightening silence. "Hush now."

She almost hissed the last words at me. And I pulled away from her. What made her talk to me as if I were two years old? Then I looked at her again. She stared down the platform, her lips tightening, her chin trembling. I looked at what was coming off the train.

Soldiers. But not soldiers laughing and running. Nurses helped these men climb down off the train, and then other soldiers supported them as they hobbled toward us. One man limped on crutches, his leg bandaged to the knee. Another with no left foot, his leg swinging uselessly. Four men shuffled by, each with his left hand on the shoulder of the man in front, the first man led by a nurse. All wore thick bandages over their eyes.

I moved back, away from them.

Not a sound but shuffling feet.

These men looked like the pictures in the paper, except this wasn't a drawing. These men had to struggle to walk. Some seemed to have trouble breathing.

Then men in wheelchairs were rolled down the ramp by nurses pushing them from behind. Again, they passed us silently, more slowly still. These men too were bandaged and wrapped: heads, eyes, arms, feet. Some slumped into their chairs, blankets wrapped high under their chins.

One man's body ended at the knees. Another man coughed all the way down the platform. The nurse behind him kept one hand on his shoulder as if to keep him from slipping out of the chair.

Then, right in front of me, a man began to shake suddenly, to shake so hard that the blanket covering him slid off his lap. The nurse bent over him, tucking and patting. I watched her in fascination. How could she touch him? I heard her murmuring as she bent above him. What could she say to him?

She patted him once more and then paused to readjust her veil. I looked at her face, calm, not horrified at the man shuddering in front of her. Without once looking at us, she pushed him on. All the nurses were the same, serious, calm, all attention on the men in the wheelchairs in front of them.

I glanced at my mother, but she wasn't looking at me.

Another nurse stepped down from the train and motioned to someone behind her. A tall man in uniform backed out of the train, holding the ends of a stretcher. Another man followed, balancing the other end.

"Stretchers," I whispered.

As the first one passed by us, I looked at what was on it. I saw a man, a blanket pulled to his chin. His eyes were closed, his nose flattened and twisted to one side, only a mass of bluish skin where his mouth should have been. A hole at the side of his face moved in and out as the man on the stretcher breathed.

The men carrying the stretcher stopped, waiting for the way to clear. I could not look away from that face. And then he opened his eyes and looked at me. In all that ruined face, his eyes, clear brown eyes like my own, were still all right. He could see me. And because he could see me, I tried to smile at him.

Then the stretcher-bearers moved ahead, but as he was carried away, the man on the stretcher kept watching me, moving his eyes and then his head just a little until the crowd came between us.

I closed my eyes and covered my face with my hat. But I could still see those eyes looking at me from that mass of pain. I began to tremble.

Suddenly I felt my mother leave my side and move forward. I stood still, my eyes closed against what I might see next.

"Annie, look who's here," my mother said, and I felt myself gathered into a different darkness, one of rougher texture and sharper smell.

"Hello, my love." It was my father. I looked up, saw his face, felt his hands brush back my hair. Mother reached over me to touch his cheek.

"Katherine. And Annie. Oh, it's good to see you both." And he hugged me to him again. I stretched my arms around him.

But even my father, solid, whole and healthy as he had always been, could not block from my sight that parade of wounded men behind him.

6

2

The sun was hot as I walked with my parents to the car. I climbed in the backseat, folding Father's uniform jacket across my lap. Father set his heavy bag under my feet and then got in beside Mother. I clutched the bright daffodils Father had bought for Mother, their fragrance mixing with the odors of tobacco and rubbing alcohol from my father's coat. I wondered to myself if they would last the twenty-mile drive home.

My knees bumped against the front seat, and I realized I had never sat in the back of this car before. I had always sat next to Mother, where Father now sat. And my legs were too long to fit comfortably. Now that Father was home, I would have to get used to being crowded.

As we drove past the warehouses that lined the river, I noticed that Mother's hands trembled on the steering wheel. Father had never seen her drive, and I knew she wanted to impress him. He didn't seem to notice.

The cool air riffled my hair and brushed my hot cheeks. I leaned my head against the side of the car. Mother and Father were talking, but the wind in my ears made it hard to hear more than a few words. I heard Mother say "Paul" several times and knew she was talking about the day we had heard he was dead. I remembered the sound she had made as she read the telegram and the look on my grand-father's face when he came back to the house from the shed where he had chopped wood for an hour after the telegram came. And I remembered how my grandmother wouldn't leave her room for three days, but lay in the darkness and cried.

The men at the station. Did their families know what had happened to them and how they would look when they got off the train? What if Paul had come home without a leg, or blind . . . or like the man on the stretcher? I looked down at the daffodils and took a deep breath of their pale scent. That face. I still saw it . . . still saw him.

I looked at my father's back, at his blond hair below his uniform cap. At my mother, her dark hair coiled low on her neck below her hat. Just then Father turned and smiled and winked at me. Before I could smile back, he turned away.

I had cried on the ride home the day Father left. Uncle John, Paul's young brother, had driven and Mother had sat beside me, patting my hand. After the first few days, we didn't talk about how we missed Father. Mother didn't speak easily of her loneliness. She kept our routine, saw her friends, played her piano, helped my grandparents. But I watched her as she read the first letters from my father, as she folded away his clothes, as she held his shirts to her face before packing them away in the cedar chest. I knew, or thought I knew, how much she missed him.

I missed Father too. Our house seemed bigger and quieter without him. I missed him especially in the evening, the time he would come home from the hospital and I would run to meet him as he walked up the street from the trolley stop on the corner. That hour took the longest to pass in the years he was gone, as I sat on the porch watching the day darken or lay upstairs in my room reading. That was when I most missed his arms that surrounded me completely in a hug and his warm laugh that coaxed me to tell him my secrets.

Mother and I had grown closer in the time he was gone. We talked more than ever before, about the family, about books, about the animals I loved so much. We spent many evenings writing long letters to Father, decorated with my sketches of my dog and Mother's cats. I wrote him about school, what the teachers said about the war, about my friends and enemies on the playground.

Once a week the postman brought us a letter from him, usually only a page, sometimes less. Then Mother would say, "Your father sounds tired." He never told us about the hospital or about his patients. Now I knew why.

And now he was home. Here with us. No more letters. No more lonely evenings. Mother drove slowly down the main street of our town and then turned down our street. The high elms made patches of shadow over the hood of the car, and several neighbors on the street waved to us as we passed. They all knew Father was coming home today.

Mother turned into our driveway, tires crunching over gravel. And all the family was there. My grandparents waited on the porch with Aunt Felicia and Uncle Mark. Uncle John ran out to the car and then stood shyly by as Father climbed out. Father shook his hand and then hugged him. Everyone stood back a moment and then swarmed about my father. My cousins, Frances and Charlie, hung on his arm and Grandmother began to cry as she reached up to hug him.

I stood by the car, still holding the jacket and flowers, and watched them. I wanted to run and hug my father again as my cousins had done. I wanted to hold his hand as my grandmother did. But I wanted him to call me, to hold out his arms to me as he used to. But he seemed too busy with everyone else to notice me. Finally, everyone moved up to the porch, John carrying the bag, Grandmother clinging to my father's arm.

Grandfather called to me by the car. "You coming, Annie?"

"Yes." I fumbled with the car door, trying to close it without trapping the coat or crushing the drooping flowers. Grandfather lifted the coat from my arms and slammed the door.

"Come on, let's join the party." He pinched my ear gently. "You're the one your dad wants to see most of all. Let's go, quick as a train."

Inside the house, all was confusion. Fidelio, my dog, pranced about my father's feet; my cousins stampeded the kitchen where Aunt Felicia was cooking dinner; John tried to light the fireplace while Grandmother fretted that it was too warm for a fire.

Father stood in the middle of it all, Mother beside him, looking around the living room, from the piano by the big windows to the stairs arching into the shadows.

"I'm home!" he announced finally and, turning to my mother, kissed her. John whooped, my cousins cheered and my grandfather kissed my grandmother. Still holding the daffodils, I knelt by Fidelio and squeezed his warm, woolly neck. He licked my cheek and patted me with his tail.

After the first burst of happiness, some of my own shyness seemed to rub off on my cousins. They hid in the hall, watching my father as he stood in the kitchen drinking iced tea and kidding my aunt. She had pushed Mother out of the kitchen, saying she'd see to dinner today.

Mother sat on the porch, talking with my uncles and

grandparents. Uncle John leaned against the porch railing, smoking and flicking the ashes into the bushes below. I could see this annoyed Grandmother, but she didn't say anything. John had been too young to be drafted and was angry that the war had ended before he'd had a chance to go. After Paul died, Grandmother worried over John and got very upset when he talked about enlisting when he was eighteen. Now he worked in town and was growing a mustache like Paul's.

I sat on the steps, listening to all the talk, feeling an emptiness in this day I had so looked forward to. I wondered if everyone felt it.

When Father came out of the house, I hoped he would sit by me on the steps, but he eased down beside Mother on the porch swing.

"The house looks fine," he said to my grandfather. Everyone looked at the porch roof that Grandfather had painted last week. "I'm sure that's a lot your doing."

"Yes, we all pitched in to help Katherine. Didn't want you coming home to a ruin."

"Thank you. Even the yard looks good."

"It's early yet, though. Grass hasn't had a chance to dry up," Grandfather replied, looking out over the green lawn.

They all looked into the pale sun and seemed grateful for the chance to look somewhere other than at each other.

I looked from face to face. How could they talk like this, about the grass and the house. Didn't they realize that now everyone was here, safe at home, everyone but Uncle Paul? And no one seemed to remember except me.

"Why . . . ?" asked Mother.

"Where . . . ?" interrupted Uncle Mark. They laughed a bit and everyone got up quickly when Aunt Felicia called us in to dinner.

Grandfather stood waiting until we were all seated and

quiet and looking at him. Then he bowed his head. Silence moved over the table. I crept a finger over the bumps on Mother's best lace tablecloth and waited for Grandfather's customary "Our Father." But today the words were new ones.

"I thank You, our Father, for the safe return of Lawrence. And for bringing the war to an end . . ." Silence for a long moment. "For this family. Bless us and strengthen us"—now the words were familiar ones—"to do Your work on earth and to prepare us for life everlasting."

Then, before he could close with "Amen," another voice, my grandmother's voice. "Bless dear Paul. Bless him and keep him in Thy care."

I lifted my head and looked at her where she sat at the end of the table, her hands clasped in front of her as she bent over her plate. And I saw my father reach across and cover her hands with one of his as my grandfather said, "Amen."

We ate ham and watermelon pickles and corn pudding and Father's favorite vegetable, lima beans. Everyone talked about family and local politics and church finances. I didn't think I wanted to eat, but when the steam rose from the plate Aunt Felicia passed to me, I realized I was starved. Bowls and platters were passed, water glasses filled. Then I noticed that neither of my parents ate much. Mother drank a lot of iced tea and Father pushed his food around on the plate. Once he grinned at me when he caught me giving a piece of ham to Fidelio, who always begged at the table.

After dinner we all helped clear and John mentioned croquet. Suddenly, everyone wanted to be outdoors. John set up the wickets while Charlie and Frances pounded in the stakes. Uncle Mark leaned back on his mallet and puffed his cigar, smoke curling up over his Panama hat. Aunt Felicia trailed about the yard, examining Mother's roses, and had to be called from the back lot so the game could begin.

"Come on, Annie," called Frances. "You be on our team."

"Yeah, you're good." Charlie swung his mallet at the grass. "Come on!"

Both my cousins suddenly seemed very childish to me, even though Frances was only one year younger than I and Charlie only two. Standing out in the hot sun, squinting against the light, they both seemed like babies, and I didn't want to be part of their game.

"No. You go on. I'll watch," I called to them.

Frances folded her arms and stuck out her lower lip and Charlie made a face at me.

"Annie." Mother spoke quietly. I didn't look at her because I knew what she was going to say. "Annie." Her tone was sharper so I turned. "You should go play with them. They're your guests."

I shook my head. "I don't want to. I'd rather stay here." Then I turned away. I heard her say my name again, but I ignored her, and soon she started talking to Father and the others and forgot about me.

I leaned back against the porch railing and watched the game. My cousins and Uncle John soon defeated Uncle Mark and Aunt Felicia, but not without a lot of noise: my cousins squealing and laughing, Uncle Mark bellowing, Aunt Felicia screaming whenever her ball was knocked away. I was more than ever glad I had stayed on the quiet porch.

Grandfather rocked slowly while Grandmother knitted. Mother stroked Muffin, her favorite of all the cats, and watched Father. He sat, hands clenched behind his head, staring out over the yard to the Russian olives that bordered our back lot. No one said much but pretended to concentrate on the loud game going on in front of us. The afternoon wore down.

"Well," said Aunt Felicia, coming up on the porch mopping her bright face. "We must be off. You'll want some time alone." She went to my mother and kissed her on the forehead. "Lawrence looks tired. Don't let him go back to work too soon, Kate."

It took them a moment to collect hats and to call in my cousins. Finally they were gone.

The day was still light but fading fast. A cooler breeze came in from the west, moving the trees in the front yard. Fidelio was a golden shape as he trotted up the street on his night errands.

My father was in the living room, looking out the window. While Mother and I put away the dishes, he stood there, silent. On my way between sink and shelves, I took quick peeks in at him. He was so quiet, almost sad, not jolly as he used to be.

When we had finished, I started up the stairs to my room.

"Annie," Father called to me, his back still to me.

"Yes?" I waited, hand on the banister.

"Let's have some music." He turned and sat on the heavy couch facing the piano. "Come sit with me." He patted the pillow beside him. "This is what I have waited for."

Mother stood in the door to the kitchen, silhouetted against its light, drying her hands on a towel. She walked to where Father sat, leaned over and kissed his forehead. She waited while I walked slowly to the sofa and perched hesitantly next to Father, then she circled me with her arm and pulled me close to him.

"What do you want to hear?"

"Anything. I just want to hear you play."

I don't know what my mother played. The notes had no distinct tone but melted together and poured over Father and me as we sat in the evening light. I leaned my head against his shoulder and he held my hand. The silver pitcher of daffodils on the piano held the last light of the day in the warm, darkening room. Mother played until she could no longer see the keys and then she brought a stool to sit by Father's side. We stayed there in the quiet warmth until I fell asleep.

3

The next day was Saturday, but I woke early anyway. I lay in shadow for a moment before I remembered what had happened the day before and then it all came tumbling over me: Father, the station, the wounded men, the face on the stretcher, that man's eyes . . . I shut my eyes a moment and pressed my hand over my face.

The sun crept up the bed and over my hand. I turned and opened my eyes. Uncle Paul looked back at me from the picture on my dresser, the picture he'd given me just before he left. Not a stiff formal pose like the one on Grandmother's mantel, but one that showed my uncle laughing, head to one side, rumpled dark hair shading one eye, a wide happy smile that showed his teeth and made him look like Mother.

I sighed and lay still a moment, looking at him in the early light. Then I jumped out of bed. I expected Father to be still asleep, but he was up and gone when I came downstairs. I was almost glad. I was used to having Mother to myself in the morning and was not yet ready to share her.

She was at the piano, where I usually found her. "Hello, Annie." She turned and smiled at me. "You're up early." I stood beside her as she smoothed my hair back from my forehead.

"Where's Father?"

"He went across the street. Your grandfather came over early and asked him to take a walk." She looked out through the lilac bush to the street. "He was up so early. I don't think he slept well."

She rose quickly and closed her piano book. "Come on. I can't seem to get anything done today. Come and have some breakfast."

In the kitchen she brought me a blue bowl filled with strawberries.

"Mother?"

"Hmmm?" She reached up to the cupboard for a cup and poured herself coffee.

"Yesterday at the station. Those men . . ."

She turned and looked at me where I sat, not eating.

"What, Annie?"

"That man on the stretcher, with the face . . . and all the others. Do you think they'll ever be normal again? Will they be all right?"

She reached across the table and circled my hand with fingers warm from the coffee cup. "Of course they'll be all right. The war is over and they're home again. You don't need to worry about them." She smiled at me and took a sip of coffee.

"But they're so badly hurt. That one man . . ."

Mother set her cup down with a clatter. "Forget about them, Annie. They're not your worry. I want you to put them out of your mind. All right?"

I looked at her a moment without speaking.

"Annie?"

Mother's tone told me not to question further. She stood and poured me a glass of milk. "Now eat your breakfast. We're going into town when your father gets back to buy him some new clothes. Nothing fits him. I never thought he would lose weight, but he has." She sighed.

I ate slowly and watched my mother move about the

kitchen. She was usually graceful and I thought she looked like a queen: tall with long arms and hands, hair coiled on top of her head. But today she seemed nervous, picking up dishes and putting them down, spilling sugar into the sink. I was sorry I'd mentioned the men at the train. Maybe she couldn't get that face out of her mind, either.

Then she leaned to look out the window over the sink. "Here's your father now, down at the corner. And your grandfather."

I hurriedly finished my milk. "I'll go meet them." I ran out into the pale morning before she could answer and saw Grandfather and Father still at the corner, standing and talking. Fidelio looked up from his browsing in the grass and galloped to meet me, then danced around me, delighted with his morning run. I swung my arms as I walked and watched my father and grandfather. They were both big men, tall and handsomely built, as Grandmother always said. Grandfather was old and looked frail next to Father, but he still stood straight, his gray head almost even with Father's.

Father wore the old clothes that had hung in the basement, forgotten when Mother packed everything else away. They did look too big. But he looked more like my father, now that he'd taken off his uniform. His gray pants and white shirt rolled up to show his strong arms and hands, his hair that always curled a little around his face, his brown eyes—this was the father I remembered. Then he reached out with one arm and drew me to him. "Good morning, love. Why aren't you getting ready for school?"

"It's Saturday, Father. Don't you know what day it is?" I laughed and hugged him.

I could almost reach around him with both arms. He had lost weight. Or I had grown.

He slapped his forehead. "Of course. I lost track. I thought you were playing hooky."

Grandfather bent to kiss me on the forehead. "Beautiful day, Annie. Time you were up." His mustache tickled my face.

"Grandfather, it's only seven-thirty."

"Half the morning's gone by now. You've missed the best part of the day."

Father chuckled. "Annie's growing. Needs her sleep." He squeezed my shoulder and we began to walk toward the house, Fidelio padding in front of us.

"Well, I think it's a fine thing, James," my father said. "Timothy was a bright boy." Father paused a moment. "Wasn't he quite a baseball player?"

"First baseman. Good arm." Grandfather nodded and then sighed. "Oh, well."

"Often this blindness is reversible. Don't give up hope for him." Father dropped his arm from around my shoulder. "You remember Timothy Lewis, Annie? Lived next door." He nodded to the low green house next to my grandparents', across from our own. "He's out at St. John's, the hospital where they're sending the wounded who can't go home yet."

Timothy Lewis. He and his friends had played baseball on our street all summer long and he had had a dog that once bit the milkman. His parents had moved into Kansas City years ago, so I didn't remember much more about him.

"What happened to him?"

"He's blinded, temporarily most likely. Should be all right in a bit." He smiled down at me. "Your grandfather's been going out to read to him. *Ivanhoe*, isn't it?"

Grandfather nodded. "Nothing like Sir Walter Scott to

19

stir up the blood. I think Timothy enjoys it. Says he does, anyway."

"Is that where you go when you tell Mother you're going to visit an old friend?"

He grinned at me. "Right you are. Your mother would not approve."

I glanced at Father and saw him tighten his lips. "Why not?"

"Well, let's just say that my daughter has strong opinions. And sometimes she has trouble keeping them to herself. You're a brave man, Lawrence Metcalf."

Father laughed. "Well, Katherine and I have this worked out, I think. I broke the news to her by mail two months ago, and she's had time to get used to the idea." He turned to me. "Annie, I'm not going back to County Hospital. I'll be working at St. John's now, with the wounded men."

"You mean the ones on the train yesterday?"

"Those. And the ones already there, like Timothy Lewis. I've had some experience with them and I want . . . I want to go on working with them."

"What does Mother say?"

"She'd just prefer that I stay on at County Hospital."

I wished my father would stay at County too. Didn't he want to get away from those men, now that he could, now that the war was over? My grandfather too. I tried to picture Timothy, blinded. I stooped and picked up a willow branch that had fallen on the sidewalk and I switched the picket fence in front of the Wilsons' yard. Grandfather and Father walked on ahead of me and I looked at their backs. I didn't understand how they could walk through the sunshine laughing and talking when they knew they would have to go out to that hospital and look at that man with no face. When maybe Uncle Paul . . .

I whistled to Fidelio and ran as fast as I could to the corner. When I got back, they were talking about what to put in the summer garden. They didn't mention St. John's and wounded men again.

Mother came out on the front porch and shaded her eyes against the morning light. "How was the walk, Larry?" she called to Father. "Everything the same?"

"Yes and no." Father rubbed his hands through his hair as he climbed the steps. "It's all the same, I guess, but it seems so quiet. No crowds, no noise."

"After New York City, I can see why." Mother waved to Grandfather. "Let's go. Maybe downtown will make you feel at home. You want to drive? Or do you trust me?"

Father grinned at her. "You drive. I've forgotten how."

They left the porch, laughing, arms around each other. I sat for a moment, a wave of warmth coming over me. Maybe it was the morning sun streaming through the mock orange and onto the porch, but I think it was the sound of their voices, the look of my father in his old clothes, and his grin. I gave Fidelio a brisk face-and-ear rub and then ran to follow my parents.

We stayed up late that night, playing dominoes, eating the chocolates we had bought in town. The windows to the porch stood open and cool air drifted the light curtains around the piano.

I left my parents there when I went up to my room. I sat by the window, listening to their voices from below, Father's rich baritone, Mother's laugh. It sounded good, their voices together. Maybe Mother wasn't happy about Father's new job at St. John's, but if she felt the way I did, it didn't matter. It didn't matter where he went when he left us in the morning because we knew he would come back to us in the evening.

I wound my braid around my head with one hand. Father was home; the uneasiness I had felt yesterday had vanished in the laughter of our trip to town. Why then did I still feel a wash of sadness over me? Why couldn't I laugh like my parents were doing downstairs? Why did I want to sit in the shadows of my room?

I heard my father come up the stairs. He stopped a moment outside my door and I watched him against the light.

"Annie? Are you asleep?"

"No, I'm awake. Come in, Father."

He pulled my old rocking chair over to the window and eased into it. "Been a long time since I sat in this and read you bedtime stories."

"I know. I used to love that. Father, I'm so glad you're home."

"I am too. So, how's my girl?"

I swallowed, unable to speak for a moment. I pleated the filmy curtains between my fingers and then smoothed them out on my lap. Suddenly I knew what was troubling me, what I had to ask Father.

"Annie? Something wrong?"

"No, not really. But I've been wondering about those men at the station, your patients." I stopped, but I didn't look at him.

He reached out and put his hand over mine. "Is that bothering you?"

I nodded.

He sighed. "I don't know what to tell you, Annie. You know those men were wounded in France."

"Like Uncle Paul."

"Yes."

"But he died."

"They were luckier than Paul. He was killed outright. No chance for him."

"Do you think he looked like that . . . like the man I saw on the stretcher?"

"No, Annie. I'm sure he died quickly. Don't worry. He didn't suffer."

I had never thought of Uncle Paul suffering, being hurt, until I saw those men at the station, those men in so much pain. Not until then did I think about what might have happened to my uncle.

"What happened to those men? The one I saw . . . He was so ugly, like his face had been smashed."

"Different things. Some were burned, hit with phosphorus shells. Some were shot, some hit with mortar shells or shrapnel. The ones you saw today were too sick to travel right away, so they were kept in New York to recover before coming home." He paused. "But Annie, understand, we are trying to make them as well as we can. The worst is over for them. They are no longer in great pain. They're the lucky ones."

The slow parade of wounded passed again in front of me. Lucky? My father had never lied to me before. But I knew he was now.

"Please believe me, Annie. I know it looked bad. But they are closer to home now, near their families. And they're happy."

I wanted to laugh out loud. How could he say those men were happy? Did he think I hadn't really seen them? Or that I was a child to be soothed with a pretty story? I turned away. I couldn't look at my father's face. He would see, even in the darkened room, that I didn't believe him.

23

Father spoke again. "Annie, I almost wish you hadn't been at the station to see those men. But we'll all have to live with them around us. So you just got an early taste of what we all have to accept."

Now I looked at Father. His voice had changed. He seemed to have trouble speaking. "And we have to, somehow . . ."

For one moment he covered his eyes with his hands. He didn't speak. Then he straightened. "I must do all I can for them, Annie. All I can. That's all I know."

I leaned over and put my arms around his neck. I wanted to tell him that I believed him, that I accepted the lies he told me, but I couldn't. I couldn't believe that the worst was over for them. And neither did my father. He had come home to us, but also to them, and if he was going to spend his days treating their terrible wounds, then, I resolved, I would have to learn to look into their faces.

4

Father brought warm days home with him. Overnight, the lilacs bloomed and the peony buds by the front porch grew fat. One of the outdoor cats that I fed on the back porch had four kittens.

I went back to school and to Darby and Emily, my two best friends.

Father began work at St. John's, across town, and Mother went back to her music. She wrote music, stacks of it that lay in piles under the piano. Most of it was for the piano, but she also wrote songs, music for poems she especially liked. She had given lessons when I was a baby and Father was just beginning to work and we were poor. But she didn't have the patience for teaching, she claimed, and hated to hear miserable playing ruin glorious music. Gradually, her students dwindled away, and everyone was relieved. She didn't even teach me, for which I was grateful. I loved to hear music, but hated to play.

Father once said that if Mother were forced to choose between her music and her family, there would be a long pause while she decided what to say. And even then, he said, he wouldn't want to bet a month's salary on her answer.

When I was very young, I had learned not to interrupt Mother when she was at the piano. I learned to play alone or to cross the street to my grandparents', where I was always welcome. Now that I was older, I loved to stay in my room or out on the porch and listen to her play, or to sit on the steps and watch her sway and move with the sounds she made. She forgot everything when she was surrounded by music.

Before the war, Mother had had two groups of friends. One group was all women, friends from the academy she had attended before she and Father were married. These women played and sang together, but mostly talked, sitting in our living room, their voices low and earnest. Sometimes they read articles from the paper out loud or passed around books and papers for everyone to read. Some of them were writers, some teachers, some musicians. They all believed in votes for women.

Father always went to my grandparents' house on the nights they came. But he was very polite to the women and I think he respected them, because he told me once that he hoped I would have their intelligence and honesty when I grew up. I liked them too, very much. They treated me as an equal, talked to me seriously about school, asked my opinions about things and gave me suggestions of books to read.

Mother's other group of friends had first come to our house with Uncle Paul, who was a student at the Music Academy. He and his friends, all about twenty years old, called themselves "serious musicians." Father called them Mother's "boys." Mother said they needed encouragement and a place to be themselves. They loved music, loved playing and singing. There were seven of them, and when they came, they filled our living room with sound: their laughter, quick words, the crashes from the piano when they played their new compositions.

Mother didn't allow them to smoke in the house, so they stood on the porch and in the summer the smoke drifted in through the open windows. In the winter, I could see them through the glass on the front door, shivering violently, puffing at their cigars and cigarettes.

I didn't particularly like them, because they either ignored me or called me cute names. They all looked alike to me in their dark jackets and tiny mustaches. Except Uncle Paul.

When I remember Mother's boys now, two years later, all I can think of is Uncle Paul. His is the only face I see. He looked like my mother—tall and dark, and usually serious. But when he smiled, his face broke into circles of laughter. For years he hadn't paid much attention to me because I was so much younger. It was John, my youngest uncle, who played with me. Only four years older than I, he used to read to me, and when I was little he let me follow him down the street to play. But Uncle Paul wore elegant suits and brought girls who wore their hair up to family dinners. He went away to college for a year and then came home to attend the Music Academy.

Like Mother, he wrote music, strange music that he played on the piano with great seriousness. I didn't really like what he wrote, but I always clapped hard when he finished. I liked it better when he sang, especially popular new songs like "When I Leave the World Behind" or "When I'm Out With You." I pretended that he was singing just to me where I sat in the shadows of the stairs.

He came to our house a lot to talk to Mother, especially when he'd had an argument with Grandfather, who wanted him to stop writing music and find a "real" job. Mother would listen to him thoughtfully; Father would tease him a little and then go back to his paper. I wanted to tell him not to listen to my grandfather, that I thought his music was magnificent. But he never asked me. He never really noticed me except to pat my head or give me a distant "Hi, little Annie."

But one night, a month before he left for the war, that

27

changed. Mother was next door when I heard the doorbell ring and then someone call, "Katherine! Anyone home?"

When I turned on the porch light, I saw Uncle Paul, twirling a key on his finger, his hair tousled and wild, a grin lighting his face. "Annie, is your mother home?"

"No." I stepped out on the porch. "She's next door."

He peered through the lilac bushes at the lights splashing out onto the lawn. "Oh, darn. I wanted to show her . . ." He turned suddenly and grabbed my hand. "Come on, I'll show you. I'm dying to tell someone."

He pulled me with him and together we ran down the path, across the street and down my grandparents' drive. I gasped for breath, clutching Uncle Paul's hand as we ran. He stopped by the shed in the backyard, bent over me and put one finger to his lips. "Shh, be very quiet now. It's in here."

I didn't know what to expect, but the cool night breeze on my face, the darkness around me and my uncle's mysterious excitement made me giggle, caused my breath to catch in my throat. I shivered as I watched him open the door to the shed and step inside.

"Where is it . . . ?" I heard him mutter, and then an arc of light swept the inside of the shed. I saw a motorcycle leaning against the wall. Uncle Paul moved the light down its length, lighting bits and pieces of leather and metal.

"Isn't it a beauty? Just look at it!" He smoothed the seat with his hand.

"Oh, yes! Is it yours?"

"All mine." He switched off the flashlight and wheeled the motorcycle out into the yard.

"When did you get it?" I circled the motorcycle, poking my finger between the spokes and feeling the bumpy tires.

"I picked it up this morning. It's the latest model Harley-Davidson. It can do forty, fifty miles per hour." He ran his hand around the headlamp. "I'm tired of poking along on buses and trolleys. You think your mother would like to ride this?"

"Oh, can't you see her on it, wearing one of her big hats?" I leaned against the handlebars and laughed. Uncle Paul swung his leg up and over the seat and then looked at me.

"Want to come for a ride?"

I backed up. "Really?"

"Sure, it even has a seat on the back for you. Climb on."

I swung into the seat that rested on the back fender and put my feet up on the little steps. I wrapped my arms around Uncle Paul and turned my face, resting my cheek against his warm back.

"All set? Here we go."

He stepped down hard and the motor exploded into sound. I bounced on the seat as we drove out over the rutted drive into the street. Then the ride smoothed as we came out on the paved road. Uncle Paul drove slowly down our street and I wondered if people looked out from their lighted rooms to see who was riding a motorcycle in the dark street. We passed a few people walking, and several dogs jumped out on the road as we came by, then ran up onto the curb to bark and chase us.

The night was close around me, the trees loud in the wind overhead, every rock and rut in the road right under my feet. The breeze curled around my uncle and snatched at my hair and blouse, and I was afraid that it would pull me off the bike. I hugged him harder.

Then he turned onto Centre Street, lined with the stores where Mother shopped and Town Hall and my school. Now I felt everyone staring at us as the overhead lights on the corner glowed around us. We zipped around the few cars that were out and I saw faces looking out at us from the windows. When he stopped at a corner, Uncle Paul steadied the bike with both feet and peered over his shoulder at me.

"OK, Annie? You like this?"

I could only nod. My breath was gone. I heard him laugh and then we were off again.

I had dreamed of flying and I knew this would be the closest I could ever come. The noise, the trees whipping past us, the cold air pushing at me, forcing even my laughter down my throat and making it hard to open my eyes, and all the time my uncle sheltering me behind him.

When we finally circled the block one last time and turned into the drive, I was exhausted with excitement. I could barely stand for a moment.

"I loved it." I tipped my head back and danced out on the lawn, my arms wide, the stars wheeling above me. Then I stopped and closed my eyes. When I looked again, the stars stood still and winked at me. "That was wonderful! Thank you."

My uncle leaned over the motorcycle handlebars, watching me and grinning in the starlight. "Quite a ride, isn't it? It's like, like . . ." He shrugged his shoulders.

"Flying. It's just like it must be to fly." I ran my hand along the metal that shone in the starlight.

"Right you are." He wheeled the motorcycle toward the shed but stopped a moment and looked at me again. "I'm glad I found you and not your mother. She'd just have lectured me on how unsafe this thing is. But you, Miss Annie, are a person of taste and you appreciate the value of this magnificent chariot."

Then we both laughed and Mrs. Wilson next door raised her window and glared out at us. Uncle Paul waved to her, put his fingers to his lips and we tiptoed away.

I didn't see him for a few days, but every morning and again in the evening, I heard the roar of the motorcycle from across the street. I always ran to the porch when I heard it and I always waved, but Uncle Paul, goggles over his eyes, didn't see me. I noticed other people watching him pass, older people on their porches shaking their heads and flapping their hands, children trying to race him on their bicycles. I didn't tell anyone about our ride. I didn't want anyone else to know.

Mother laughed and said that buying a motorcycle was just like Uncle Paul. "He's always been a little crazy, a little wild," she said. And then she sighed. "I just hope he doesn't go off and do something idiotic." She shook her head and left the room. I knew she meant the war. So many other young men we knew had already enlisted, not waiting to be drafted. Uncle John talked constantly about going when he was old enough. But not Uncle Paul. Not until the spring of 1917.

One night that June, he called and invited me to go to the opera with him the next evening.

"It's *La Bohème*, Annie. My favorite."

The opera. With my uncle! I had never been.

"I have an extra ticket. I hope you can come."

"Oh, yes. I'd love to."

Mother helped me get ready, ironing my best white-lace dress and braiding my hair, since she wouldn't let me wear it up. When I tried to fasten the clasp on my coral bracelet, my hands shook so hard that I dropped it.

Mother laughed as she picked it up. "Excited?"

"Yes," I mumbled. "I won't know how to act at the opera."

"Don't worry. Paul will understand." She fastened the bracelet and patted my hand. "My brother is used to taking young ladies to the opera."

"Why did he ask me? Do you think someone turned him down?"

Mother shrugged. "I don't think so. He's not seeing anyone special just now. I think he wants to go with you. Maybe he sees what a lovely young girl his niece is becoming. That's all."

I felt the same whirl of excitement that had come over me on the motorcycle, but this night was different. Uncle Paul had asked me to go with him. He wanted to be with me, not just because he couldn't find Mother. I could hardly fasten the buttons on my shoes. When I looked in the mirror, I didn't see any lovely young girl. All I saw were my hot, flushed cheeks. But at least my freckles didn't show.

Then Uncle Paul arrived in a cape lined with red satin. He laid my coat gently across my shoulders and we went out into the cool evening. As we walked to the trolley stop, he told me the story of the opera, about the love of Mimi and Rodolfo, both poor and starving but happy until they quarreled.

"But he finds her at the end and even though she's dying of tuberculosis, she is happy." He tossed the trolley fare in his gloved hand and laughed. "Quite a story, Annie. True love wins out."

The lobby of the Pantageus in downtown Kansas City glittered with light when we entered. Women in long satin dresses and men in tuxedos chattered and smiled at one another under the marble ceiling. I knew they looked at us as we passed through the lobby. Uncle Paul was the most elegant man there.

We sat in the balcony with a clear view of the stage.

Uncle Paul helped me with my coat, bought a program for me and read out the Italian names. Then the opera began and I forgot where I was. The singing was nothing like the sounds that came from Mother's Victrola. Even though they sang in Italian, Uncle Paul had told me enough of the story for me to understand what was happening. And when Mimi died and Rodolfo sang his last sobbing note, my uncle handed me a handkerchief.

"I brought an extra," he said. We sat in silence for a moment while the crowds around us filed out.

"Well, Annie, what do you make of grand opera?"

"I wish I could sing like that. So beautifully that people cry."

He nodded and smoothed his mustache. "Yes, I feel that way sometimes. My problem is I don't know whether I want to write beautiful music, sing grand opera, play the piano . . ." He waved his hand and laughed. "Or ride a motorcycle faster than anyone else. There's so much I want to do." He sighed and cocked his head at me. "Father says I'm not serious enough about things, about life. That I need to be making plans and settling down." Riffling the program, he looked out over the empty seats in front of us, his eyes serious. "What do you think? Should I sell my motorcycle and buy a Model T? Give up my music and sell shoes?"

He was so serious, so unlike the man who had laughed with me in the moonlight. He looked over at me. He was waiting for me to answer, as if he really cared what my answer would be. I thought of my parents, Mother with her music and Father with his job. They both were doing what they wanted, what they loved.

"Don't sell your motorcycle. It's wonderful," I said softly. "So is your music."

"You really think so?"

I nodded and looked up at him. "Yes. You should do what *you* want to do. I don't think you'd be happy selling shoes."

He murmured, "No, I don't either." He straightened in his seat. "Do what I want to do. Good advice." Then he stood up and, taking my hand, pulled me to my feet. "Thank you, Annie. You're a wise young lady. I'm so glad you could join me this evening. For many reasons."

"I am too. Thank you."

I thanked him again when he brought me to the door of our house, thanked him and told him I would never forget this evening. And then he kissed my hand, just as Rodolfo had kissed Mimi's.

Mother was waiting for me in the living room. When I told her about the opera and was unable to explain how wonderful it all was, she said she knew.

"And how was Paul? Did he treat you all right?"

"Oh, yes. He acted like I was . . . like I was a lady."

Mother tipped back her head and laughed. "How nice of him. Paul has his faults, but he is a gentleman. I tell you, Annie, there are advantages to having such young uncles. You'll appreciate it before you're much older."

But Uncle Paul enlisted in the army before I got much older. The next week he announced that he was going. Had I influenced him? Probably not. One of his good friends had been drafted, he said, so the whole group decided to enlist to keep him company.

Mother's boys had one last night at our house, three of them already in uniform. They sang the popular war songs, "Over There," "It's a Long Way to Tipperary," "Smile, Smile, Smile." They talked louder than usual that night and laughed constantly.

Uncle Paul talked and laughed with them and sang

34

every song. But I watched him all evening and saw him look around the living room several times as if he had never seen it before. I noticed him rub his hand along the black curve of Mother's piano. I watched him pat Fidelio more than he usually did. And he came and sat beside me on the stairs and put his arm around me as he sang. Before he left, he told me to write, to take care of my mother. Then he stooped to kiss me on the cheek and he whispered, "Good-bye, little Annie." The screen door banged behind him and he went out with the others, walked out into the night, still singing. From the window by the piano, I saw Uncle Paul turn on the walk and blow me a last kiss.

5

Summer came. No school to get up for. Days of time to spend as I wished. Dreary Monday and joyful Friday were the same in the summer heat, only Sunday keeping a special feeling. Father, Mother and I found our summer routines.

I saw Emily and Darby occasionally, but without school we had no one to talk about, and for the first summer of our lives, our regular games seemed too much trouble in the heat. So we got together and sat and waited for something to happen. And nothing ever did.

June limped along and I was alone most of the time. As I did every summer, I spent hours reading in the backyard or in my grandparents' cool basement when the chiggers drove me indoors. Once a week, I went to the downtown library and came back loaded with books—stories and atlases and books about foreign countries.

I had learned to love maps from Ruth Sylvester. Ruth, about ten years younger than Mother, was small and dark and wore sober skirts and blouses, just the opposite of my tall, beautiful mother in her big hats and silk dresses. Ruth was also quieter than Mother. I noticed she didn't let the whole world know how she was feeling, as Mother did. In spite of all this, Ruth and Mother were friends, and Ruth had also become my friend. She lived alone and worked in the town library, two things I thought were very glamorous. I wanted to be just like her, to campaign for votes for women as she did and to read the thick magazines I saw in her house.

One night about a year before the war started and everyone went away, Mother's friends were at our house and Ruth found me where I had perched, as always, on the steps. She sat beside me, gathering her long skirts around her, and then opened the large book she held on her lap.

"This just came into the library today. It's splendid. Look, Annie. Bombay. Ceylon." She slowly turned the pages. "Honshu. Chosen." More pages and she pointed to names on the bright splashes of color. "Damascus. Constantinople." She rolled out the name, lingering over every sound. "Oh, I dream of going to all these places. Do you know"—she laughed and hugged the book to her—"I even plan how long I'll stay, what I'll take, how I'll get from one place to another. I know it's silly." She opened the book again and balanced it on her knees. "And then I go to the newspapers." She looked at me and grinned. "And I look up the shipping schedules in *The New York Times*. Just to see when the next boat leaves for Hong Kong." She pointed to a dot on the underbelly of China. "Or Madras." I looked at India where it dipped gracefully into the ocean.

I smoothed the page with my hand and looked at her. "It is beautiful. Maybe you'll go someday." I grabbed her hand. "Let's go together."

She smiled and nodded. "Someday."

I began to dream of taking such trips after that first talk with Ruth, of drifting down the rivers I traced on the maps, of meeting veiled strangers in Kashmir or Samarkand, and they would never have seen someone like me and they would take me to the palace to meet the prince and . . .

After Uncle Paul left, I began to study the map of Europe more carefully. I found Le Havre where he would have landed, the Somme River near where he was based, Paris and the Île de France. And my dreams changed. Now I was there in France, a nurse helping the wounded, risking death to care for a soldier with dark eyes.

And then he died. And I put away my maps. I didn't want to find the place where he had been killed. Instead, I looked at books of photographs of Europe and read about the palaces and cathedrals that I was sure had nothing to do with the war.

Grandmother worried about me and told my mother that I should have more company. "The child will turn solitary and strange," she said. "She needs good solid friendships at her age."

"Annie makes her own company," my mother answered. "Besides, she has all the animals."

"Hardly the same, Katherine. Dogs are to be seen and petted, not spoken to."

I laughed when Mother repeated this conversation to me, but inside I was annoyed. Grandmother still treated me like a child, still thought she knew best what I did and did not need. And it wasn't company I needed. Darby and Emily were close by, and my cousins. I had plenty of people around me. But this summer was different. My books and dreams weren't enough. Since Father had come home, my dreams about going to Europe seemed silly, and thinking about Uncle Paul only made me wish all the more that he had come home.

One afternoon I found Grandfather dozing on his front porch and I suggested a game of checkers. He seemed glad, even when I beat him.

"I shouldn't have taught you so well." He chuckled as he set out the pieces for a rematch.

"I'll let you win this one." I rocked slowly in the heat.

Then I sat up a bit straighter. "Grandfather, how's Timothy Lewis?"

"Oh, doing as well as can be expected, I suppose."

"Can he see?"

"Nope."

I rocked a bit. "What's it like out there?"

"At St. John's?" Grandfather reached in his back pocket for his handkerchief and wiped his face. "Oh, it's a pleasant-enough place. Lots of trees and shade."

"I mean the men. What are they like?"

Grandfather looked out into the yard, squinting into the sun. He folded the handkerchief thoughtfully before he said, "Just a lot of badly hurt boys, Annie."

Badly hurt boys. The shaking man. Would he sit in bed all day? Grandfather said trees and shade. Maybe he'd be outside. Or the man with a foot missing. Could he get outside if he wanted to? He'd had so much trouble walking. The man on the stretcher. What would he do all day? Maybe someone came to read to him, too.

I tried to picture St. John's, to see myself there as I had dreamed myself into the hospitals in Europe. But it didn't work. I could imagine palaces and temples but not how Grandfather's badly hurt boys spent their days.

Father talked about St. John's. Every night when he came home, we sat on the porch and he told us about his day. He mainly talked about the nuns who ran St. John's. He called them "crackerjack nurses," some of the best he'd seen. I didn't know much about nuns. Father had never worked with them before and I had no Catholic friends. They seemed a bit mysterious with their veils and convents, but Father said they were friendly and funny at times.

One evening he told us about getting lost on the second

floor of the hospital. He was looking for the laboratory and opened a door onto a long dark hallway.

"I knew immediately I was in the convent," he said. "Suddenly, out of the darkness appeared"—he paused and puffed on his pipe—"a nun. A great tall nun with great long sleeves like wings. And"—he puffed—"she had a broom. She waved it at me—and I went!" Father chuckled, and Mother and I looked at each other and laughed.

Gradually, almost hesitantly, he began to talk about the men and I began to ask him questions.

"Mail call is the high point of every day. They all gather in the center hall around noontime every day and wait for it."

"Do they get many letters?"

"Not enough."

"Well, do people come to see them?"

"Not many. Oh, some—parents, brothers and sisters. A few. It's hard, I know. Hard for everyone. But most of them are pretty lonely."

"So what do they do all day?"

"Many of the men have treatments. Therapy. Otherwise they read or play poker—endless poker games. They listen to the gramophone. Or sit. A lot of them just sit."

Once in a while, he would say, "Sergeant Smith went home today" or "Lieutenant Peterson's wife came to get him today." But that didn't happen often.

Whenever we talked like this, Mother got up and left the porch, saying she had to see to dinner or the dishes. Father would always pause a moment and then go on talking to me.

It made me angry that Mother didn't stay to listen, because Father seemed to want to talk about the hospital, seemed to enjoy telling me the stories about his patients. One evening I asked him why she always avoided our talks about St. John's.

"Well, Annie, your mother has never been much interested in hospitals. As a matter of fact"—he shifted in his chair and leaned back—"she never has visited me at work." He smiled at me. "She . . . well, she just has other interests."

"But I'd think she'd want to know about your work."

"She doesn't expect me to love music the way she does. And I don't expect her to be interested in what I do."

I knew it wasn't the same thing. Father loved Mother's music and tried to understand and listen when she talked about it. But I could tell he didn't want to say any more about her.

"Father, I've been thinking a lot about St. John's lately. And the men . . . your patients."

He looked at me. "I thought so. Even the ones who upset you that first day?"

I nodded. "But they seem funny and nice when you talk about them. I want to know how they're doing. Could I visit the hospital someday? I promise I wouldn't be in the way or bother you or any of the men. I'd really like to."

My hands were clenched in my lap. I realized how much I wanted him to say yes.

He looked out over the darkening yard, smiling a little.

"I don't see any problem with that. You could come out with your grandfather. He'd like that." He nodded and looked at me. "No problem. But your mother would have to agree."

At first she didn't, saying, "Absolutely not." But after Father said her name quietly and they looked at each other a long moment, she threw the tea towel down in the sink and said I could go, if Grandfather agreed. And we all knew that he would.

Once everyone had agreed, I almost wished I hadn't mentioned going. Especially when Grandfather said he was going the next day and would love to have me come along. I almost told him I couldn't, that I had other plans. But I was afraid that then I'd never go. I felt the way I did the day Father came home, wanting so badly for something to happen but not sure how to act when it did.

I sat at my window that evening, listening to night sounds: dogs barking, cicadas scraping, a piano from down the street, people talking on the porch next door.

Why *did* I want to go to St. John's? I made myself remember once again those men: that leg swinging with no foot, that helpless shaking, that face with no mouth. I might see any of those men tomorrow.

I didn't really know why. I only knew that since the day Father came home, since I had seen those men get off that train, I couldn't forget them. Maybe if I just went out once, I wouldn't have to go again.

So my grandfather and I set out the next day with library books in my bookbag, Father's lunch in a picnic basket, and Sir Walter Scott under Grandfather's arm. I was going alone to the library since Grandfather didn't want to walk the two blocks from the trolley stop. He'd go on to the hospital, where I would meet him later. He patted me as I got off and told me to be careful.

The sun was hot and my bookbag heavy. I decided to take out only one book today, but when I got to the shelves behind Ruth's desk where the geography books were kept, I had trouble, as always, deciding which one. I fingered their bindings and looked at the tables of contents. The one on Europe looked brand-new, but I finally took the one about South America because of the pictures of the llamas.

When I arrived at the hospital, it was close to noon. I stood just inside the high iron fence and looked at St. John's. It sat on a small hill, set back from the road, with a path and driveway curving up to the front door. The red-brick building had three stories and looked like the manor houses in Grandmother's picture book about Scotland. To the right of the path, open lawn stretched down to high lilac bushes. Maple and oak trees shaded the grass on the left. I could feel coolness from under the trees as I walked up the path.

Then I saw the men sitting on benches and sprawled on the grass under the trees. They wore dull-gray robes and most were bandaged. A few had crutches beside them, and one or two sat in wheelchairs.

I paused in the shade, telling myself to cross the grass and ask one of them where my father might be. My mouth felt dry. Just then I saw a nun come out of the door of the hospital and walk down the path toward me. When she got closer, I saw the heavy cross hanging from the belt round her waist. She smiled and nodded to me.

"You must be Annie. I'm Sister Mary Frances. Your father said you were coming for a visit." We shook hands. Her hand was cool and dry and I noticed a ring on her finger, like Mother's wedding ring.

"Just let me see to Dick's dressing. Then we'll find your father. Your grandfather is still with Timothy." She hurried across the grass, her skirts swinging around her black shoes.

I walked slowly up the path and sat on the bottom step. Sister Mary Frances walked among the men, patting some, moving one man in a wheelchair out of the sun, pausing to watch a checker game for a moment. Then she stopped by one man, lifted the bandage taped over his eye and replaced it with another she pulled from her pocket. She spoke to him for a moment and then turned back up the path.

"Come this way, Annie." She opened the door of the hospital and we stepped into a cool hall. I stopped a moment to let my eyes adjust to the darkness after the bright sun. Then I saw two men sitting in wheelchairs just inside the door.

"Look who's come for lunch with Dr. Metcalf," Sister Mary Frances said to them. "His daughter."

"Hello," I said, a bit too loud. They looked back at me without speaking. They were covered to the waist with blankets and their hands lay motionless in their laps. They were pale, their eyes shadowed in the dim light.

I followed Sister Mary Frances down the long high-ceilinged hall. At the end of it I saw my father, standing with another nun, looking at some papers in the light from a tall open window. He turned and smiled at me, his eyes crinkling as they always did, while he bent his head to hear the nun's quiet voice. Sister Mary Frances patted me as she had done the men on the grass, nodded to my father and whisked off into a room opening off the hall. Before the door closed behind her, I saw a row of beds, most of them empty, and high windows open to the shady park outside.

I turned back to my father and found him watching me.

"How do you like St. John's, Annie? Did Sister show you around?"

"No, I just got here," I said, handing him his lunch. "We didn't have time."

"Tell you what," he said, walking me back down the

44

hall, his arm around my shoulder. "Let's rescue your grandfather first. He's had enough of *Ivanhoe* by now, I'm sure. We'll eat out on the veranda. Then you two can look around on your own while I finish up here and we'll go home together. I can leave early today."

He stopped by the door through which the nun had gone. Another just like it stood opposite. "These are the wards. Off limits to you, I'm afraid. But the men are mostly outside anyway. And you can go anywhere else, except upstairs. The convent, you know." He grinned at me.

I took a deep breath. "OK." It all seemed very pleasant. Except for the men at the door.

We found my grandfather sitting on a bench in the shade, his thumbs hooked in his suspenders. He was alone. Timothy had been called for treatments but would come back after lunch. They'd had time for only one chapter, an exciting part, Grandfather said, and Timothy wanted to find out what happened at the tournament between Ivanhoe and the black knight.

We followed my father onto a shady covered porch furnished with tables and wicker chairs. He swept one of the tables clean while I laid out the lunch. Grandfather eased himself into a chair and wiped his face and smoothed his mustache.

"I can tell you made this and not your mother," Father said. "This looks delicious."

I was pleased. Father always said he married Mother in spite of her cooking.

We chattered on through lunch. I told them about my trip to the library and showed them my new book. Father teased me about my reading habits and said I would put the library out of business. We didn't mention the men or the hospital.

When we had finished and packed up the cups and

napkins, Father leaned back in his chair and laced his fingers behind his head. Grandfather's head began to drop onto his chest. Father and I looked at each other and smiled. We both looked out at the lawn in front of us and the men scattered about under the trees. Suddenly I realized how quiet they were, even the men playing cards or checkers. No one laughed or called to one another. No one swore as Uncle John and his friends did when they played poker. But Father had said these men were happy.

I thought of all the noise I had made through lunch and I glanced at Father, my face growing hot with embarrassment. He too was looking at the men but with such sadness that I forgot my own feelings. I watched him, hoping he would return to his playful mood. Then he turned to me.

"So, Annie. This is St. John's," he said quietly and nodded toward the men under the trees. "Glad you came?"

I didn't answer. I didn't know yet.

"Why don't you walk around a bit, see what you want to see and I'll find you in an hour or so. All right?" He glanced at Grandfather. "I'll wake him in a bit when Timothy's ready."

"Do the patients mind if I walk around? Will I bother them if I talk to them?"

"Hard to say. Some may resent it, but they'll let you know. Some aren't very friendly, others are. I trust you to know what is the right thing."

He reached across the table and squeezed my hand. "Just remember, most of them, all of them, have been through more than either of us could imagine. And seeing a girl like you might cheer them up."

Then he left me. I picked up my bookbag and walked out onto the grass, leaving the picnic basket on the table and Grandfather snoring in his chair. I didn't know where to go. I wasn't sure I was ready to meet any of the men, or talk to them, in spite of my father's reassurances. Maybe I could just find a place to sit and read until Father and Grandfather were ready to go home.

I looked across the path and noticed a wooden bench with a high back facing out over the open grass. I could sit there a moment and collect my thoughts. As I walked toward it, I pulled the atlas of South America out of my bookbag. I could spend the time looking at it. I crossed the path, hopped down a slight incline and rounded the bench, dropping the bookbag over the high back.

Someone was already sitting there. He turned.

I felt as if I had been hit in the face. For a moment I couldn't breathe.

The only normal thing about him was his eyes, but even they were pulled out of shape. The rest of his face was red, as if it had been deeply sunburned, and all of his features were pulled downward, as if hot tears had run down and melted his face. His mouth had no lips. It looked as if someone had cut a slit where his mouth should be.

We stared at each other, I holding to the back of the bench, he half-turned away from me.

He wore a gray bathrobe over pajamas like the others, and his brown hair was cut short. He looked young, huddled there on the bench in the sun. I thought of Grandfather's words—"badly hurt boys." But his face.

I wanted to turn and run away, not in space, but in time, to the moment before I had seen him.

And then I did run, back up the slope, across the path, under the shadow of a tree. And I stood there, covering my eyes again, just as I had done at the train station. I stood, my hands clenched in front of my eyes, waiting for the image of that face to fade.

Then I heard footsteps on the path. What if it was Father?

What if he found me here? I dropped my hands, took a breath, and opened my eyes. A nun walked down the path, not looking at me. What had I done? What was he thinking, that man on the bench? Father had said that these men had been through more than I could ever imagine. And I, despite my brave words, could not look one of them in the face. I had run away like a silly child.

I looked around. No one seemed to have noticed me. The quiet men under the trees, the nuns walking among them, no one was looking at me. I could find Grandfather and tell him I wanted to go home. Then I remembered I had left my bookbag on the bench. I had to go back and get it. I had to, even if that man was still there.

I pulled down my blouse and pushed back my hair. Then I walked out into the sunlight, across the path, down the slope and around the bench. I'd just do it. Get it over with.

He was still there. My bookbag lay on the bench beside him. He turned. Again, we looked at each other.

"I left . . ."

"What do you want? Come back for another look?" His rough voice caught on the words.

"No . . . I . . . no." I couldn't catch enough breath to speak.

Suddenly he stood up and the robe fell loosely around him. He put his hand on the back of the bench and I saw that his hand was shaking. I stepped back.

"I don't mean to bother you, but . . ."

"You have. Go away." Every word scraped his throat.

"I just came back to get my book." I stared up at him a moment and then bent to pick up my bookbag. "I didn't mean to bother you, really." I straightened and looked at him. Again, I felt like I had been hit, only more gently this time.

"Good-bye," I said.

He looked at me a moment, his slit of a mouth turned down, his brown eyes wide open in the bright light. Then he sat down, slowly, wrapping his robe around him. I saw white bandages where his fingers should be.

I turned and left.

6

I sat in the back of the car, my books in my lap. Fortunately, Grandfather and Father had been absorbed in discussing Timothy's progress all the way to the car and had ignored me. I was glad, because I couldn't talk about what had happened, how badly it had all turned out.

I wasn't good at this. Mother was right. I shouldn't have gone to St. John's. And I wouldn't go again. Even meeting Timothy and seeing how much he liked Grandfather hadn't helped.

It took Grandfather longer than usual to get out of the car and he leaned heavily on Father's arm for a minute as they stood by the door.

"I'll walk you over, James," Father said. "I want to take a look at Paul's motorcycle, anyway."

Paul. I sat in the backseat of the car, alone. Oh, Uncle Paul. What if you had been sitting on that bench in the sun, waiting for the day to end?

After dinner, during which St. John's was not mentioned by any of us, Father asked me to come with him while he checked his tomatoes. "I want to know about your afternoon. Are you glad you went?" He ran his finger over a new green leaf.

"Oh, it was OK, I guess." I kicked at a dirt clod and wished I could tell him. "I didn't do much."

"Hmmmm, sounds exciting."

"I did see one man. His face is, well, it looked . . . burned. Red and pulled out of shape."

Father nodded. "We don't have too many with burns. Most burn patients didn't make it this far."

"How was he burned?"

"Well, I'm not sure, since I don't know the man you saw. But he was probably gassed." He knelt down and crumbled a clod of dirt between his fingers. "That's the cause of most of the burns we see."

"What does that mean?"

Father sighed. "Most of our men were burned by mustard gas. It's a kind of poison. The Germans dropped it in shells or canisters on our troops. The gas exploded and burned whatever was around, especially human flesh. Hands, faces—whatever the gas touched. Men died right away if they breathed in enough. The gas masks were supposed to help. Sometimes they did."

Father squatted back on his heels, his hands hanging loose. We both watched a grasshopper edge along the vein of a leaf.

"Did we do it to them?"

"To the Germans? Yes, we did."

"The man I saw looked awful."

Father didn't say anything.

"And his voice sounded scratchy and sore."

"Did you talk to him?"

"Not really. He . . . he didn't want to talk."

"Yes, well, I can see why." Father stood up and dusted off his knees. Then he stood, hands on his hips, and looked out over his tomatoes. "We'll just have to learn to deal with things like that, things the war left behind."

A few days later, on the first Wednesday in July, our Sunday School teacher was taking our class to the Royal Theater in downtown Kansas City to see *Broken Blossoms*, a new motion picture starring Lillian Gish.

"They're bribing us to be good at Bible School," said Darby. "To make us be good examples for the little kids." He sang the last words and danced his hands in the air. Emily giggled and slapped at his hands. I watched them in the shadows of Emily's porch, where we were waiting for Miss Peterson to pick us up in her car. I had gone to Bible School with Emily and Darby every summer since I was eight. We memorized Scripture, carved wooden whistles and waded in the stream that ran through the camp. The last two summers, all of us, even the boys, had knitted socks for the soldiers. The prickly wool had clung to our damp fingers and none of the socks looked very smooth. But they would be warm. We stayed the two hottest weeks of summer and by the end we were brown, tired and saturated with silly songs and jokes that drove our parents crazy until we forgot them. For Emily, Darby and me, this would be our last summer at Bible School. Once we turned fourteen, we would be too old to go.

But now this summer I wasn't sure I wanted to go. Bible School seemed like a waste of time.

"We'll be good, won't we, Annie?" Emily smoothed her plaid skirt over her knees.

I stood up and let my skirt drop around my legs. "Look, Mother's letting me wear my skirt longer." My white pleated skirt fell well below my knees. I twisted back and forth a bit, making my skirt spin around me.

"Just when the skirts are going up! You should see the new dresses from New York. The skirts are up to here." Her hand skimmed her knees. "I saw them in Mama's *Vogue*." Just then we heard the hoot of Miss Peterson's car and we three headed out into the sun. She had the top of her Model T down, and we all laughed as our hair blew around our faces. In town, Miss Peterson parked along Grand Avenue and we followed her around the corner. Emily and I clutched each other's hands when we saw the words *Broken Blossoms* curling across the theater's marquee in Chinese lettering. We lingered in front of the posters of Lillian Gish, hair bound on either side of her face with jeweled ribbons. Behind her stood two men, one with a whip and the other dressed in Chinese clothes. When the rest of the class arrived, we girls giggled into the theater, the boys in knickers and bright white shirts walking seriously behind us. We were all stunned into quiet by the magnificence of the lobby with its plush seats like thrones and the staircases covered in red velvet. Miss Peterson asked if any of us needed to use the "ladies'," and then we filed into the dark heart of the theater and waited for the opening sounds from the organ in the orchestra pit. When Emily whispered that she'd never seen anything so magnificent, I thought that it wasn't as beautiful as the Pantageus and it smelled of popcorn.

After the first chords died away, the opening titles flashed on the screen and Miss Peterson read them in a clear soft voice. Emily nudged me and we laughed into our hands. Our teacher continued to read, just loud enough for all ten of us to hear. She read in a high voice for Lillian Gish and tried to deepen her tones when the father's words came on the screen. For the Chinese character, she used an odd accent that made Darby groan.

Emily whispered in my ear, "Does she think we can't read?"

I shrugged, but even Miss Peterson reading the movie titles couldn't ruin the story for me. I sat, my hands clenched in my lap, wrapped in Lillian Gish's loveliness and helplessness in the face of her father's brutal beatings. When the Chinese man tried to help her and was kind to her, I hoped the movie would end happily. But then her father found her again and beat her savagely. During that scene, Darby leaned over to me and whispered, "I'll bet old Peterson is sorry she brought us to see this."

We all wept as the words "The End" rose over Lillian Gish's lifeless body. Even Darby rubbed his eyes before the lights came up and the organ played its last chord.

Miss Peterson stood up in the row ahead of us. "Well, children, ice cream? I think we all deserve some after *that*." And she reached up to repin her hat to her massive bun of hair.

Blair's Ice Cream and Candy Parlor was cool and smelled of candy. We filled three tables. Emily and I tried to sit with our friends but couldn't ignore Miss Peterson's shrill request for us to join her. She ordered for all of us and then took out a handkerchief and wiped her face and throat. "Oh, so hot outside."

She asked each of us how we liked the movie and agreed with us that the Chinese man was the kinder of the two men. "He obviously was a Christian. Or had heard of our teachings." She turned and looked at me. "By the way, Annie, I wanted to ask you. I've heard your father has left County Hospital and is working out at, what is it, St. James? It's Catholic, isn't it?"

"Yes, it is Catholic. It's called St. John's."

"Well, you know I think the world of your father, but I don't see the reason for a good man like Dr. Metcalf to associate with Catholics." She looked at the others at our table as she spoke and then back at me. "Aren't the men out there in a lot of pain?" She didn't wait for an answer. "I don't know but it would have been better if they had died in Europe." She shook her head. "And so awful to look at."

I suddenly felt very hot and my stomach lurched. "They're not awful. Once you talk to them they're quite nice. Some of them." My voice died away. Timothy was nice. But that other man?

Miss Peterson glared at me and then smiled. "Yes, dear. I'm sure that's what your father has taught you to believe. We all feel sorry for them too, I'm sure."

Emily was fiddling with her spoon. I nudged her and she looked at me and smiled. Then the waiter arrived with our ice cream.

As we left the ice cream parlor and waded through the heavy afternoon heat to Miss Peterson's car, Emily and I linked arms. "Oh, that Miss Peterson makes me so mad. To say what she did about Father."

Emily swung my hand. "Why *did* he go out there to that place?"

"Do you mean to St. John's? To help those men. Just like he went to New York to take care of the wounded men from France."

"Yes, but Annie, that was different. That was the war! Now the war is over. We can all forget all those horrible things now. He could be helping normal people who can get better. Mama says those men out there will never get any better. Besides, it's true, those men *are* scary to look at, aren't they?" She gripped my arm as she whispered the last words. I pulled away from her.

She was right, they were scary. They had haunted me for weeks and I had run away from one of them. But it sounded so mean the way she said it.

"And I know your father is the best doctor in town." Emily laughed and put her arm through mine again. "That's why he shouldn't waste his time with . . ."

"He's not wasting his time! They need him!"

55

Emily drew away from me and brushed wisps of hair out of her eyes. "Well, I'm sorry, Annie, but Mama agrees with Miss P. We don't understand how your father can choose to work with those men at that Catholic hospital when he's needed elsewhere. And I don't see any reason for you to get mad. It's just the truth. Better for you to hear it from me. It's what everyone is saying."

Her words made me so angry that the heat inside me joined the burning sun and I felt I might faint right there on the bright sidewalk.

"Come on, we can't keep Miss Peterson waiting. We can't be rude."

I didn't say a word on the way home, other than to thank Miss Peterson for a lovely day and to mumble good-bye to Emily and Darby. As I got out of the car, Emily grabbed my hand and whispered, "Don't be mad, Annie, please." I looked at her. "We'll have fun at Bible School, won't we?"

I didn't answer her. I had decided I wasn't going to Bible School that summer. I had better things to do.

7

Mother and Father were sitting in the backyard under the shade of our giant elm tree, holding glasses of lemonade. Mother looked hot and tired as she hugged me and asked about the movie.

"Did Lillian Gish die at the end? She usually does."

Father fanned himself with a book. "I think she's a honey. My ideal woman. Frail and sweet."

Mother glared at him and then dropped her head back against the chair. "You and my father both. You can have her."

"Well, I'll bet she wouldn't be out campaigning for the vote like some women I know."

Mother sighed and muttered, "Men!"

Father laughed.

I patted Fidelio and then went inside to change out of my long skirt and good shoes. The house was hot, and my blouse stuck to my skin as I pulled it over my head. In the bathroom I doused my face with cold water and combed my hair off my face. I looked in the mirror. Such an ordinary face. Too healthy-looking, not exotic like Lillian Gish. My eyebrows were too pale, my cheeks too round. Too many freckles. I sighed. Back in my room, I draped my long socks over the rocking chair by the window and wiggled my bare feet against the warm wood floor. I loved going downtown, but the best part was coming home to relax.

I leaned out my window, my loose hair falling around

my face. My stomach began to unknot for the first time since the ice-cream store. I thought of all the things I should have said to Miss Peterson and to Emily, all the things that would have hurt them as they had hurt me. I knew I couldn't face a summer with them.

I listened to my parents' voices and heard Mother laugh. They both seemed in a happy, relaxed mood, so now would be a good time to tell them what I'd decided. I pulled on a loose shift that was the coolest thing in my closet and padded down the stairs in my bare feet.

Through the screen door I saw the paper boy take aim and fire the evening paper onto our porch. I picked it up and took it out back. Mother lay back in her chair, her hands hanging down on either side and Father was engrossed in his Sherlock Holmes again. I stretched out on the grass between them and rubbed Fidelio's ears.

I cleared my throat. "Um, I don't think I want to go to Bible School this summer."

Mother lifted her head and looked at me. Father lowered his book.

"Why, Annie?"

I shrugged. "I don't know." I pulled up several tufts of browning grass. "I just don't want to. It seems . . . sort of . . . childish."

I looked up in time to see my parents look at each other. Mother said, "Frankly, I'm not surprised." Then she cocked her head and looked at me. "Did something happen today? Did you and Emily have a spat?"

"Not really. But I think I'd like to be by myself this summer." I hoped I sounded casual. "You know, I spend all winter with them and then all summer too. I'd rather be here at home."

Mother shifted in her chair. "Well, I don't want you to get bored."

"Don't worry. I won't need entertaining."

Mother smiled at me. "You seldom do. You're very resourceful."

I glanced at Father and saw he was looking at me over the top of his book. "Is my little girl growing up? Too big for jump rope and jacks?"

I shook my head and grinned at him. "You're the one who always tells me to drink milk and get lots of exercise."

He reached down and rubbed the top of my head. "Just don't go too fast. Hey, is that the paper you're sitting on?"

"Oh, I'm sorry. I forgot." I handed him the front section of the *Kansas City Star*, keeping the comics for myself.

"Well, look here." Father whistled. "It's been signed. They've done it." He held up the paper so Mother and I could see it. Heavy black letters spelled out the words: WORLD PEACE SIGNED AND SEALED AT VERSAILLES.

"So President Wilson got his treaty." Mother leaned over to see the paper.

"Yes, but he has to get Senate approval, remember. That's another story." And Father pointed to another headline: LEAGUE OF NATIONS DENOUNCED IN SENATE.

"I thought the war ended last November," I said.

"The fighting stopped then. This treaty decided the final details—what lands are given up, who has to pay costs, who is to blame. That sort of thing."

"Who is to blame?"

"I don't know, Annie. Hard to say. Germany, mostly."

"Oh." I pulled out more grass and sprinkled the tufts on Fidelio's head where he lay stretched out in front of me. "Will this make the men at St. John's glad?"

Father shrugged. "Maybe. But all the treaties in the world won't end the war for them." He shook the paper out and went back to reading the front page.

So. Father had told me that the war was over for those

men. They were home. Lucky and happy. He *had* been lying.

Mother stood up. "Well, I'm glad they've signed the treaty. I hope now we can put it all behind us and go on with life." She pushed her hair back. "Oh, I hate this heat. Come on, Annie. Let's fix dinner. Any peas in your garden, Larry?"

After dinner, Father and I washed the dishes while Mother practiced some new music she'd just bought. When I told him what Miss Peterson said about St. John's, he just sighed. Then he said, "A lot of people feel that way, Annie. A lot. Just don't let it bother you." He turned to look at me as I polished a glass. "Is that why you don't want to go to Bible School?"

"Sort of. Also because Emily says she agrees. And that everyone's been talking."

"Emily too. That's hard. But you stuck up for me?"

I nodded and he touched my nose with a soapy finger. "That's my girl." Then he shook the soap off his hands and wiped them on a tea towel. "Let's finish up and go see your grandfather. He's letting me have Paul's motorcycle to get back and forth to work. Leave the car for you and your mother."

I carefully set the last glass on the cupboard. For a minute I couldn't turn around and look at him. Paul's motorcycle. His magnificent chariot, he'd called it. I wanted to cry.

"Annie, come on. You'll love it."

I didn't love seeing the motorcycle in the shed covered with a dirty sheet. All I could think of was how Uncle Paul had loved it, how he'd rubbed the gleaming metal and laughed across the handlebars.

Father and Grandfather stood looking at it in the fading evening light, hands on their hips.

"Let's get it out and see if it's still in running condition," Father said, and wheeled it out, felt the tires, looked in the gas tank. "Everything in good shape. He took good care of it."

I shivered. Yes, he loved it. And he didn't have it very long.

Then Father climbed on the motorcycle and kicked down on the pedal. The motor grumbled sluggishly.

"Needs work, I guess." He sat back on the seat. "Well, if you and Mary are sure, I could certainly use it."

Grandfather waved his hand. "It's yours. John has his own, and we sure can't ride it. I'd like to have it used." Grandfather put his arm across my shoulder.

"When I get it fixed up, I'll take you for a ride, Annie," Father said.

I shook my head. "No, I don't want to."

"Scared?" Grandfather asked. "Paul always said it was safe."

"No, I'm not scared." I hugged my arms around me.

"His goggles should be in here somewhere." Grandfather poked around in the shed. "Can't seem to find 'em. Maybe he took them with him."

"That's OK. I'll get some of my own."

I wanted to scream, they were so calm. Only the motorcycle, leaning sadly on its kickstand, seemed to remember Uncle Paul. They were chatting as if he had just left town for a vacation.

They started toward the house, and I reached out and ran my hands along the handlebars. I remembered everything.

"Annie?" Grandfather called. "You coming out to St.

John's with me next week? I'll be going on Monday."

I smoothed the leather seat.

"Timothy wants to see you again." I'd found Grandfather and Timothy after I left the man on the bench. Timothy's red hair still lay on his head like a smooth cap and his hands were still freckled, but his eyes were covered with a heavy white bandage. He'd smiled when Grandfather told him I was there and moved over on the bench so I could sit beside him. Together we'd listened to my grandfather read about the knights and their horses plunging down the lists in fierce combat.

I turned and saw both men standing on the back porch, watching me.

"Any problem, Annie? Don't you want to go back?"

Now I could say no. I didn't have to go back. But . . .

Father came down the step toward me. I turned back to the motorcycle and I nodded. "OK, Grandfather. I'll go." I turned and looked at my father. "I want to go back to St. John's." I hoped he couldn't see the tears in my eyes.

8

I loved the Fourth of July. It was in the midst of summer and meant picnics with Grandmother's delicious food and a parade downtown with the high-school band and horses. And the Fourth meant fireworks. I loved fireworks, but Mother and Fidelio hated them. When he was just a puppy, four years before, Fidelio had spent his first Fourth of July under Mother's chair. That's when Mother decided we should change his name from Thor for "Thunder" to Fidelio for "Faithful One" after a character in an opera.

But even with Father home, I didn't feel my usual holiday joy on the Fourth, almost a week after my visit to the hospital. Mother was busy all day in the kitchen getting ready for the picnic downtown, and Father spent the morning out at St. John's. I wondered if the patients did anything special, if they waved flags and sang "Columbia, the Gem of the Ocean." And fireworks. If they scared Fidelio, who'd never heard a gun go off, what would they do to men who'd been burned in explosions?

"Annie? Where are you?"

"On the porch."

"Run across and see if your grandmother needs help. It's about time to load up the car."

As I stood in the doorway of my grandmother's steamy kitchen, I hoped the men at St. John's would at least eat well today. But I knew they wouldn't eat as well as we would. My grandmother loved to cook.

I remembered her from my early childhood as a strong,

happy woman, always in the kitchen, singing the old Scottish songs she loved. She was not large, but she seemed to fill a room with her noise, her music and her constant talk, her clatter as she prepared and served food to the family.

After Uncle Paul's death, she had seemed the same after the first bad days. She emerged from her bedroom, tidied the house from the company and the disorder left by John and Grandfather, hung the black wreath on the door and draped a black ribbon around Uncle Paul's picture on the mantel.

But she didn't sing anymore, something I didn't notice until I spent a weekend with them while my mother and Ruth took a trip. I couldn't tell at first what was different about their house until I watched Grandmother fixing dinner on Saturday night. She moved silently, and more slowly, about the kitchen. As I sat and watched her, Grandfather came in from feeding his hens out back. He glanced at me sitting at the kitchen table, then at Grandmother stirring a pot of soup on the stove, and then motioned me to come with him to the front porch. We didn't talk about my grandmother, but he sat with me pulled close to him and he stroked my hair and talked about the flowers and the vegetables he was going to grow the next summer.

She didn't sing much anymore, but she still could fix a meal. By the time Father came home, she had five berry pies, a pot of baked beans, two platters of fried chicken and five dozen biscuits ready to load into the car. Grandmother had asked Mother to fix the salads.

"You can't ruin those, dear," she'd said.

"Oh, Mama!" But I knew Mother was relieved.

Ruth was coming with us. Mother had called her two days ago, and I'd overheard her say sharply, "For heaven's sake, Ruth, at least come and eat with us! Pretend it's just an ordinary picnic."

I'd wondered why Ruth would object to the Fourth of July celebration, but I was glad she had agreed to join us.

The picnic was downtown in the big park near City Hall. We found friends from church, Reverend Bingham and Emily's and Darby's families. Uncle Mark and Aunt Felicia, Frances and Charlie, Uncle John with a girlfriend, all gathered around our picnic basket and Grandmother's food.

Grandmother laughed as she dished out food, but she ate hardly anything. Father patted his stomach and told her he felt like a new man. Uncle John and his girl drifted away under the trees. I played tag with my friends for a while, but soon came back to sit with Mother and Ruth.

The town band had played dance tunes while we ate, until about three o'clock, when the trumpets blew a fanfare and we all looked toward the bandstand.

"The mayor. Shhh. Children, come sit down. Hush." The crowd quieted around us as we walked toward the bandstand. My parents and grandparents were ahead of me when I looked around for Ruth. She was not standing near us, and when I looked back to where our picnic basket and cloth lay on the grass, I saw her walking away from us toward the pond at the edge of the park.

"Friends, neighbors, Americans." Mayor Evans stretched out his arms to us. "We come together today to celebrate our nation's independence, one hundred and forty-three years of freedom. But today is an extraordinary Independence Day. Not only do we remember today our forefathers and their splendid achievements so many years ago. But today we celebrate with the returned soldiers, sailors and marines."

I noticed Mother take Father's arm, and they looked at each other and smiled.

"The general citizenship will attest in no small measure, through this celebration, the appreciation of the community for the splendid record made by our men in military and naval service and will also celebrate the delivery of the world from military dominance."

The mayor leaned on the bandstand railing. All of us were silent.

"The torch of liberty that we kindled is now held high over the world."

He sounded like Reverend Bingham, his voice rising and falling with the same grand swoops.

"The mighty have been thrown down, the humble raised up, the last of the great military autocrats has been swept from his seat of power."

The afternoon sun now shone directly on us. I took off my hat and fanned my face. Several men around me were doing the same.

"Peoples who have lived in bondage or oppression, wavering between agelong despair and newborn hope, are creating and administering their own governments. It is an Independence Day we share with the whole world."

The mayor paused, and we all shifted where we stood. "But friends, today we have something else to remember. In the midst of the general gaiety, we must remember those who are not here with us to celebrate this year, those who made the supreme sacrifice that we might all rejoice in this hallowed day."

I brushed back my hair and put my hat back on.

"As a community, we owe a great debt to those heroes who, on land and sea, offered up their lives so we might be here today. Here in Kansas City, we have formed a committee of our religious leaders"—he paused and indicated a group of men behind him—"from our Methodist, Lutheran, Presbyterian, Episcopalian and Catholic churches, to begin raising money and planning the design for a monument to be built in this very park, a monument to all those who made the sacrifice in the great war just passed."

He never said "those who died."

"We have the preliminary plans drawn up, a proposed design for the monument. We invite you all to examine it and let us know if you approve. We are still . . . ah . . . gathering the names of those who should be so honored on the monument. We will soon have a final list."

Beside me, Father snorted quietly. "That'll take a while. They're still dying."

Dying? I'd never thought about it, but men probably did die at St. John's all the time.

The mayor was still talking. "We plan also an appropriate quotation, perhaps something of a religious nature." He smiled at the clergymen behind him. "We will be asking for contributions from each church and from all of you so that this monument will come from the hearts of all of us. I ask that your prayers bless this project and that we all search our hearts for guidance as to how much we each can pledge." He paused and then turned to the band director and spoke a few words. The band struck up the opening chords of "America," and we all stood and sang.

There was a moment of silence after the last note, and then the crowd broke apart and began to chat.

"Well," Mother said and put her arm around me. We all stood, looking around us.

"I want to see the monument," Grandmother said. "If

my son's name is going on it, I want to see that it's done right."

Grandfather took out his handkerchief and blew his nose. "All right, Mother. We'll all go take a look at it."

We had to wait before we could get through the crowd to the table where the plans lay spread out. People laughed and chattered to one another over the table.

Mrs. Crawford, a friend of my grandmother's, was standing in front of us. She reached back, patted Mother on the arm and spoke to all of us. "Isn't this just grand? For all the dear boys. And your blessed Paul."

I wanted to see the monument plans too. Paul's name would be there, Paul Robert MacLeod, along with all the other heroes. It seemed quite splendid to me, then.

The plans, tacked to the table, showed a stone pillar topped with a soldier standing straight, looking out from under his helmet, rifle slung behind him. The sides of the pillar were bare.

"This is where the names will go," Grandmother said, and ran her gloved finger over the paper.

Mother leaned to look, my uncles and aunt pressed around to see. Only Father stayed behind.

"Don't you want to see, Father?" I asked him as I stepped back so Frances and Charlie could squeeze in. "It's all going to be marble and granite."

"No, you look for me, Annie. I'm not much for monuments."

I looked at him a moment. First Ruth, now my father. Didn't they see how wonderful this monument was going to be? I turned back to the crowd around the table. I was going to enjoy it all.

And I did. The afternoon passed in band music, singing, more food. Then the fireworks began, arching and tipping above us, flowers and stars falling into the darkness. A last burst of color and light sent us home cheering.

"What a lovely day," Aunt Felicia sighed as I waited with my aunt and uncle and cousins for the trolley. Mother and Father had gone in the car with my grandparents. "And especially good this year with your father home."

I glanced up at Ruth, who stood beside me in the pale purple evening. She smiled at me and nodded. I almost expected her to say something, to disagree with Aunt Felicia, but she didn't. And I was glad.

It had been a good day, but as I stood in the darkness, my happiness began to fade as the fireworks had done a half hour before. Today was Friday. Only three more days and I would have to keep my promise and go back to St. John's with Grandfather. I would go. But I didn't want to. I wanted to forget that place, the way everyone else seemed to have done.

9

But three days later I packed my bookbag with my world atlas and a book of pictures of Europe. I stuck in a few apples and some oatmeal cookies that Grandmother had baked. Mother was practicing when I told her where I was going, and she just nodded and said good-bye absently. So I had no choice. I had to keep my promise to Grandfather.

When Grandfather and I caught the trolley to the hospital, the conductor recognized me. "Going to the library again?"

"No." I shook my head. "St. John's Hospital."

"You have a relative there?" He squinted at me from under his uniform cap.

"No, my father is a doctor there."

He shook his head. "I don't know. I hope I never have to go out there. From what I hear, those fellows aren't very pretty. I hear they look awful, some of them. That true?"

I just looked at him and then turned to sit beside my grandfather. I realized how people would stare at those men, people like the conductor and Emily. Or people like me, I suddenly thought as I remembered what I had done when I first saw the men at the station and when I saw the man on the bench.

I jumped off the trolley and helped Grandfather. He handed *Ivanhoe* to me and leaned heavily on the side of the trolley as he stepped down. Then he grasped my shoulder and stood for a moment, breathing heavily as the streetcar rattled off down the street.

I looked up at his face. He was sweating and very pale.

"Grandfather, are you all right?" I had trouble standing straight under the weight of his hand on my shoulder.

"Yes, just need to stand a bit." He cleared his throat and then pulled himself erect and stepped away from me. "Just had a bit of dizziness. I'm all right now."

"Grandfather, let's go back home. Please."

"No!" He stepped carefully up onto the curb and sat down on the bench that circled the oak tree at the entrance to St. John's. He leaned back against the tree and wiped his face with his handkerchief. "No, Annie." He paused to breathe. "Can't do that. We're expected." He waved his hand up the path to the hospital behind him. "Timothy counts on me. He's waiting for the next chapter of that book you've got there." He leaned his head back, closed his eyes and puffed heavily. "And he's had enough disappointment already in his life."

"But you're sick." The shadows rippled over his face.

He opened his eyes and glared at me. "No, I am not sick. Just tired. And not even that now. Come on." And he pushed himself to his feet, waved the handkerchief at me, and started up the path to the hospital.

The ground under the trees was cool and shady like before, and the men were there again, just as silent, playing their games, sleeping, staring into the shadows. I wondered if all of them sat in the same place every day or if they switched around. They all looked the same to me in their robes. Only bandages and wheelchairs made a difference.

"Timothy usually waits over there." Grandfather waved

toward two benches under the trees beside the hospital. "You run and see if he's there. I don't want to waste steps."

I glanced at his red face. "I'll stay with you."

"Go *on!*" he almost shouted.

As I ran across the grass, I knew I had to tell Father how Grandfather was acting. I found Timothy on the bench where Grandfather had said he would be.

"Hi, Timothy," I called. "It's Annie Metcalf. We'll be right there."

Grandfather marched across the lawn toward us, his back straight, his mustache shining in the morning light. "Hello, son." He put his hand on my shoulder as he lowered himself onto the bench. "It's a hot one." He mopped his face.

"Mr. MacLeod, meet Andrew Crayton." Timothy waved his hand. "Friend of mine. Andrew, say hello to Annie Metcalf."

I looked up from helping Grandfather get settled, across the shady grass to the bench that faced us. And I saw the burned man. He was looking out at me from under a hat pulled low over his eyes. His hands and arms lay on his knees, palms upward as if he were warming whatever lay beneath the bandages.

Grandfather got up again to shake his hand and then had to be settled again, so it didn't matter that I didn't say hello. But now I realized the only place to sit was beside the burned man, beside Andrew Crayton. I looked at the grass as I walked toward him, sat down carefully and dropped my bookbag between us.

"So you came back."

For a minute I didn't realize he was talking to me in that harsh voice.

"Yes."

"Your dad's the doctor?"

"Yes."

He didn't speak for a minute. I pleated my skirt between my fingers and looked across at Grandfather and Timothy, who were talking quietly.

"Do you come here a lot?" I could tell he was looking at me.

"Not really." I shrugged and turned to look at him. "Have you been at St. John's long?"

He nodded. "Four months. I got here in March."

"Is my father your doctor?"

He shook his head. "No, but I know who he is. I see him with the other guys. A couple of them are in worse shape than me. Can you believe it?" He laughed, a short sharp bark. And then he coughed. It seemed to hurt him. He brought his muffled hands up to his face but could not cup them around his mouth. He swallowed and then cleared his throat.

Grandfather began to read and we all listened. Or Timothy did. And maybe Andrew. I was too nervous to concentrate on the story. Of all the people to be sitting with! I didn't dare move on the bench for fear I might hurt him, so I sat up straight and uncomfortably. My legs began to hurt, and all I could think of was how I wanted to get up and leave. Grandfather read on. I didn't hear a word, just the sound of his voice, on and on. How long could one chapter be?

When a nun came toward us across the grass, patted Timothy's shoulder and took him away for treatment, I was relieved.

Grandfather closed the book and stretched. "I think I'll rest a bit. This story's too much excitement for an old man." He closed his eyes and dropped his chin on his chest.

I glanced at Andrew. He was looking at Grandfather, almost smiling.

"Excuse me a minute," I said and ran through the shadows to the hospital steps. I wanted to find Father. Grandfather looked better, but I was still worried. But Father was busy and only had time to listen with a frown, nod and say he'd be out as soon as he could. I wanted to run and hide from the man on the bench, but I knew I had to stay with Grandfather in case he woke up or felt sick again. So I went back.

Andrew was still there, hands crossed in his lap, head leaning against the high back of the bench. Then as I watched, he lifted his head and looked down at his hands.

I could sit next to Grandfather now, but I saw Andrew watching me, so I sat down beside him and pulled my bookbag onto my lap. My hands shook. I wished Grandfather would wake up.

"Always lug that thing around?" Andrew asked.

"Not always. My mother calls me a bookrat. I usually carry a book with me, in case, you know, I have a chance to read."

He leaned back against the bench. "Your grandfather looks tired."

"Yes, he does. But he likes to come out here. And I . . . I like to come too. It's so peaceful here."

"Peaceful, huh? Like a cemetery," he muttered. He shifted on the seat. "Might as well be one."

Neither of us spoke for a minute. I peeked up at him to see if he had gone to sleep. He hadn't, but was staring out over the grass.

"What kind do you have today?"

For a moment, I didn't know what he meant. "What?" I finally said.

"Books. What kind of books?" He waved a bandaged hand at my bookbag.

"Oh, maps. I love to look at books of maps. And dream about traveling to all the places I see." My voice died away. I usually didn't talk about my love of maps, and I felt silly doing so now. Especially to this man.

"Let's see them."

"Really? They're just maps."

"I know." He sounded annoyed. "But it's something to do."

I pulled the books out of my bookbag, sliding the cookies and apples down into the bottom, and opened the world atlas.

But he was looking at the other book, *Europe in Pictures*.

"That one." He nudged it with the back of his hand.

I opened the heavy cover and balanced it between us on our knees. A spot of sun reflected off the glossy pages and made it hard to read. I lifted it a bit so the words were in shadow.

"A look at the wonders of Europe in photographs!" I read the subtitle and turned to the table of contents. As I ran my finger down the list of countries, he reached out with one bandaged hand and tapped clumsily on the section titled "France."

"I want . . ." his voice cracked and he swallowed, "to see that."

I paused, my hand covering the page in front of me. "France?" I stared at the page. When he didn't answer, I looked up at him. I couldn't see his eyes under the shadow of his hat, only the red rippled skin around his nose and mouth. He nodded. So I found the page and opened the book to the section on France. Mounds of grapes lay on a table. A château arched gracefully across a river. People smiled. He motioned for me to turn the page. An ancient city circled with a high wall, a stone church with a steeple pointing into the sky, a palace of white marble.

"I don't remember any of that," he whispered. "Only mud. And burned trees."

I looked at the church and the people standing in the streets of the tiny village on the page before us.

"No people. The church was bombed out. I don't remember . . ."

I couldn't see the happy village. The page glared in the sun.

"There weren't any people. They all left before we got there. And no animals. They'd been eaten. The sergeant said the church was safest. But it'd been bombed. Blown apart. We slept in it anyway, what was left of it. I was afraid to sleep, afraid they'd come back."

He stopped and I slowly closed the book. I tried to imagine the church with the steeple gone.

Then he began again, that slow whisper.

"It had been farmland. When we got there, the barns were gone, fences down. Mud. Mud everywhere. And rats. I can still feel the rats running over my face at night."

I hugged the book to me.

"And then the gas . . ." He stopped and lifted both hands into the air.

I watched him, sick at what I had done with my books.

"I wasn't there long." He spoke louder now. "I was there only two months. I didn't see anything beautiful in France."

"I'm sorry."

He didn't move. The sun now shone full on us, and the

reflection from the metal buckle on my bookbag hurt my eyes.

"I didn't know. I'm sorry."

"You couldn't know. Nobody knows!" He spoke sharply. Then he stood up suddenly and walked away.

I sat without moving, the sun pouring around me. Mud. Bombed churches. Rats . . . gas . . .

Timothy returned, led by the nun who had taken him away. And Grandfather rumbled awake.

"Oh, Annie. Sorry I went to sleep on you." He rubbed his face. "What you been up to? Where's that Andrew fellow?"

I was glad he didn't stop for answers, because I didn't feel like talking just then.

"Say, didn't you bring some cookies in that pouch of yours?"

So I got them out and passed them around.

Suddenly, I felt someone behind me. I turned. Andrew had come back.

"I'm sorry." He paused and put his hand to his mouth for a moment. "I'm not much good at being with people anymore."

He looked so lost, standing there. I wanted somehow to let him know how glad I was to see him. I reached out to him and carefully touched his arm. "I understand."

"No." He shook his head. "No, you don't. Don't think that you do. Be glad you don't."

"Andrew, here, do you want a cookie?" Grandfather called.

I looked at his mouth, at the skin pulled together where his lips had been. "Can you eat them?" I asked softly.

"Break it up into little pieces." He held out one hand and I dropped a small piece of cookie onto the bandage.

He brought his hand to his mouth and tipped his head back. He chewed carefully.

I blinked quickly. He couldn't even eat oatmeal cookies easily.

"Well, gents and lady, shall we return to *Ivanhoe*?" Grandfather brushed his white shirt clean of crumbs and then opened the heavy book on his lap, his hand gentle on the green marbled cover.

"I guess so. Beats doing nothing," Andrew said. He wouldn't sit beside me again but stayed off to the side in the shadows of the trees, leaning against the bark, his knees drawn up to his chest.

But he had come back. And because he had, I would be sure that we didn't talk again of France, of mud and burned trees and the empty church. The world had other palaces and beautiful cities.

Timothy crossed his arms and leaned a bit toward Grandfather. I wondered if the bandages around his head and over one ear made it hard for him to hear. I realized Grandfather was reading louder than he usually talked. Maybe for Timothy and Andrew both.

I looked around our little group, at Grandfather and Timothy. And at Andrew. Strange that his face didn't scare me anymore.

Grandfather read on, finishing one chapter and starting another. I got tired of the hard bench and had stretched out on the cool grass beside Andrew, plucking grass. At first I didn't notice Mother when she came and stood on the edge of our little circle. Grandfather saw her first.

"Katherine! What a nice surprise! Come, pull up a bench."

Mother looked at him, at me, at Timothy, and her lips tightened. Andrew stood up and she turned and looked at him. Her face grew pale. She swung back to me. "Annie, get your things. Now."

I got to my feet. "Mother, I want you to meet—"

"*Now*, Annie. I'll meet you at the car. Coming, Father?" And she turned her back on Andrew and held out her hand to help Grandfather to his feet.

"Katherine, we're having a visit here. You remember Timothy Lewis?"

Mother looked down at Timothy, who sat silently, his head tipped back. "Yes, hello, Timothy. How are . . . ?" Her voice died away. Then she went on, briskly, "Father, I've come to give you a ride home. I can't wait."

I couldn't believe Mother was acting like this.

Grandfather looked at her a moment, closing the book. "All right, Katherine." He leaned over to Timothy. "I'll have to go now, son. I'll be back soon. Take care." Then he stood up alone, ignoring Mother's outstretched hand.

I looked around. Andrew was gone. I ran around the benches and looked up toward the hospital. He was just climbing the steps to the porch.

"Andrew!" I called to him. "Andrew!"

But he didn't turn, didn't answer, and the porch door slammed behind him.

10

By the time I got to the car, I was so angry at Mother I couldn't speak. Just when I was getting to know Andrew, she had ruined it all. She had turned her back on him, had acted like he wasn't there. My mother had been inexcusably *rude*.

After I climbed into the backseat, I leaned forward. "Mother," I began.

"Not *now*," Mother snapped. And I knew better than to go on. Driving at the best of times made Mother nervous. It was no place to argue.

But Grandfather didn't seem to care. His face was flushed and his mouth tight as he turned to her and said, "Katherine, why did you act the way you did back there?"

She turned and looked at him, and for a moment I thought how much they looked alike: red faces, clenched lips. She didn't answer for a moment and then said, "Larry called and asked me to come out and get you." Her voice was higher than usual and wavered a bit. "He said you were tired, that's all."

"But to storm in and be rude to everyone! That wasn't called for."

I listened in amazement. I had never heard Grandfather talk to my mother the way she talked to me. She was always saying that things "weren't called for."

"Me, rude? When I find my own daughter sitting by . . . And you there, as if everything was lovely. A regular tea party!"

Grandfather stared at her a moment, crossed his arms and said nothing more.

We drove the rest of the way in silence. Mother turned in our drive, and as Grandfather climbed out of the car, he leaned heavily on the door. I walked across the street with him and left him sitting on the front porch, Grandmother fluttering around him.

As I walked up the sidewalk, I could see Mother sitting on the front porch, rocking hard, her heels coming down on the wood floor every time she tipped forward. Muffin, who would tolerate almost anything to stay in her lap, perched uneasily on the porch railing, tail twitching. The cat turned to look at me as I climbed the steps.

"I want to know what is going on out there." She waved her hand out to the street.

I stopped on the steps and pulled some dried lilac blossoms off the stem and crumbled them onto the cool dirt below the steps. My stomach pitched uneasily as it always did when I was angry.

"You mean at St. John's, don't you? I was with my friends. Andrew is my friend. But you treated him like he was nobody."

"Young lady, don't you use that tone of voice with me," Mother snapped. *"Ever."* We stared at each other a long moment, and then she rose and strode to the end of the porch. Muffin disappeared over the railing into the peony bushes.

"I'm just glad I went out there or I would never have known what was going on."

"What . . ." I swallowed.

"I'm not really angry at you. More at your father. That he let you . . . When I agreed to your going out there, I never thought you would be seeing the men, other than

Timothy. I thought they would be in the wards, in beds. I never would have agreed otherwise." She turned and looked at me. "Who was that man? The one with the horrible face?"

"I told you. Andrew Crayton. I met him last week."

"You *met* him? How?"

"By accident. He was sitting on a bench and I sat down next to him. He doesn't look that bad if you take the time to get to know him."

"What can you find to talk about? He must be ten years older than you."

"My books. Today we looked at some pictures of France and he liked them," I lied. I pushed from my mind the way his eyes had stared so blankly when he started talking about the mud and the rats. "Father says they don't have many visitors out there."

"Well, that's hardly your problem. You are my concern." She looked out over the lilacs. "Annie, you can't go out there again."

For several seconds the words did not mean anything. They were only sounds. Then I realized what she had said.

Mother turned back to me. "Did you hear me, Annie?" She spoke almost briskly now. "I'm sorry, but you can't go out to St. John's again. Seeing these men, seeing this Andrew, will only upset and worry you. And it's not your job to provide company and conversation for them."

"It doesn't upset me. Honest." I beat my clenched fists against my legs. "Oh, Mother, you'll ruin everything."

She stood in front of me, her hands on my shoulders. Her hands felt hot and her fingers dug into my skin. I shook her hands away and she backed away a step.

"It may upset him to have you out there. Did you ever think of that? He's probably ashamed of the way he looks and would rather not have visitors. Not now. Maybe in time."

"How would you know that? I'm the one who knows him. You don't know what he feels. He likes talking to me." Again, I had to push aside a memory, when he told me to go away, saying that I was bothering him. I took a deep breath. I had to make her change her mind. "Mother, he likes listening to *Ivanhoe*. He's a friend of Timothy's. Grandfather—"

"I can't keep your grandfather from going out there, although I happen to think it's too much for him too." Mother paused and looked across the street. "But he's an adult and can choose for himself. You're just a child and shouldn't be exposed to all this ugliness."

"Ugliness! That's not fair!" I exploded. "I'm not a child! I'm old enough to make my own decisions. And it's not ugliness!"

Mother held out her hand.

"Annie, please try to understand. That war brought so much misery to so many people. I won't have it touching you. We've done our part, giving Paul. That's enough. More than enough. It's bad enough that your father . . ." She paused and put her hand to her forehead. "It's over and done with. We should forget it."

"That's what Miss Peterson said. They should have died in Europe so we wouldn't have to look at them. Would you like that better? So *we* wouldn't have to be upset. I can't believe you feel that way too." Now my voice shook and threatened to give out altogether.

Mother shook her head. "Annie, you must not talk that way."

"Father said you don't like hospitals. Well, I'm sorry, but I do!" Tears finally ran down my face.

"Annie . . ." Mother stepped toward me, but I turned and pulled open the screen door and ran into the house and up to my room.

11

When Mother called me to dinner, I went. I had never been allowed to be sullen or to pout, so I climbed off my bed, straightened my dress, washed my face and went downstairs. I was not hungry. Father had called to say not to wait dinner for him, so Mother and I ate in silence. She seemed to have as much trouble swallowing as I did. Soon I asked to be excused. The house seemed very hot and I wanted to go out back and be alone. Mother took her coffee out on the front porch, where a small breeze sometimes came up in late evening. We didn't speak as we passed in the hall.

I found the kittens and picked one of them up as the mother cat watched me distrustfully. The yard was dark and cool, only a faint red glow coloring the western sky. The only sound came from the cicadas, scraping endlessly.

I began to cry, letting the tears drop on the kitten's fur. In the darkness, in the solemn night, I suddenly felt very alone.

The mother cat blinked at me. I rocked the kitten a moment and then set him down in the grass. I wiped my eyes on the back of my hand. As usual, I didn't have a handkerchief when I needed one.

I tipped my head back and found the first star. My mother, who usually understood me. What had changed her? She said that seeing Andrew would upset and worry me. But she was the one who seemed upset! Yet I had to admit, just to myself, that only a few days ago, I'd wanted to forget St. John's, that I'd been afraid to go back. Oh, how confusing this all was!

The kitten mewed at my feet and I picked him up again. I had always known Mother didn't like hospitals. But maybe it wasn't just any hospital. Maybe it was only this one, where the wounded from the war were treated.

I rubbed the kitten's head with my chin until it purred. It couldn't be because of Uncle Paul. Mother had avoided the war even before he died.

She had never read the newspaper accounts of the war, and after Uncle Paul and Father left, we never talked about it at home. The day after her boys went away, she burned the sheet music of the war songs they had left on the music stand of her piano. One day, when I came home from school whistling "Keep the Home Fires Burning," she clamped her hand, hard, over my mouth and told me *never* to sing those songs again. I asked her why, but she didn't answer. I obeyed her about the songs, except in school where we began each day by standing by our desks, hands over hearts, and saying the Pledge of Allegiance, then singing a patriotic song. I always felt faintly guilty at this betrayal of Mother's command. So I hummed the tunes but didn't sing the words.

When the casualty lists began to come out in the paper, Mother never looked at them, but I did. We soon knew who had been killed. We heard from Darby's mother that Adam Franklin, one of Mother's boys, had been killed three weeks after he arrived in France. And one Sunday the minister read out the name of Henry Baldwin, the finest tenor on earth, Mother had said. She put away her hymnbook, took my hand and walked out of church during the reading of the scripture.

Maybe she couldn't bear to think about the war or anything about it. And the hospital and the men who lived there were all we had left of it now. I closed my eyes and lifted my face to catch the cool air. The kitten squirmed and I put him down where he and his sisters, all awake now, walked awkwardly about in the scratchy grass, putting paws down gently. Their mother lay on her side and watched them. I took a deep breath and stretched my arms over my head to the sky. The night was quiet around me.

Suddenly I heard voices in the street. Then lights came on in the kitchen. A minute later the back door slammed and I saw Uncle John run to the garage and begin cranking the car. I stood up.

"Annie!" Mother's voice.

"What?"

She didn't answer. I patted the mother cat and ran to the back door. No one was there. Through the hall, I saw the front door open. I ran to it and saw Mother running across the street to my grandparents' house. Grandfather! I ran after her. At the top of the steps she turned and saw me.

"Go home, Annie. Call St. John's and tell them your father must come home. Then call Mark and Felicia. Go."

"What's happened? What do I say?"

"Your grandfather. Like the last time. He's sick. Go!"

I turned and ran down the steps.

"Annie!"

I looked back at her.

"Stay there after you call. Don't come back." I looked at her standing in the front door. All I could see was her silhouette against the light inside. I ran home.

The nun at St. John's said she'd tell Father immediately. Uncle Mark and Aunt Felicia weren't home, so I called Ruth. She'd be able to help.

Ruth was home and said she'd be right over. After I hung up, I remembered that she didn't have a car. She'd have to ride her bicycle in the darkness. Just then I heard Uncle John call my name from the hall.

"Did you get your dad?"

"Yes. He's coming."

"I've got the car ready. We have to get Dad over to County. We can't wait."

"Wait for Father. He'll know what to do."

"Can't!" John called over his shoulder.

I stood in the hall a moment. Then I ran out the front door and across the street, up the steps of my grandparents' house. I stopped at the door. My grandfather lay on the sofa, Grandmother holding his hand, Mother bathing his face with a cloth. His eyes were closed, his mouth slightly open. One of his hands hung loose over the edge of the couch.

"Grandfather," I whispered.

Just then I heard our car pull up to the curb and then the sharper sound of the motorcycle. Father was here! In the pale light on the street, I saw him drop the motorcycle on its side and then run up the steps, two at a time, his black bag in his hand. He brushed by me. Uncle John came in from the back and stood brushing his hands through his hair, over and over.

I slipped out onto the porch, where I sat on the swing. I held my elbows with both hands because suddenly I felt that if I didn't I might fly apart. I heard voices from inside, mostly Father's and Grandmother's. She was crying. Then the front door banged open and I saw Father and Uncle John step out, my grandfather's arms around their necks. Father talked softly to my grandfather as they eased him down the steps and down the dark path to the car.

I stood up and went to the steps. Mother ran past me, a blanket in her hands. I followed her. She leaned into the car, tucking the blanket around my grandfather, who lay stretched out in the backseat. Suddenly Ruth stood beside me and her arm was warm around my shoulder.

"How is he?"

Mother straightened and saw her. "Oh, Ruth. Thank God. How . . . ?"

"Annie called me. How bad is it?"

Over the roar of the car starting, we couldn't hear what Mother said. Ruth shouted, "Go on. I'll stay here." Then she helped lift my grandfather's head and shoulders so Mother could slip in beside him. Father climbed in beside Uncle John and the car swung out into the street. We stood and watched its taillight bob down the street.

I shivered and Ruth hugged me to her. "How's your grandmother?"

"I don't know. She was crying."

"I don't doubt it. You go on in. I'll put my bicycle out back and be right in. She'll be a handful, I imagine."

And she was. We spent the evening trying to calm her, fixing her tea, hearing the story over and over of how my grandfather came in from feeding the hens and fell to his knees in the kitchen, how she dragged him to the living room and up onto the couch. She cried and blamed herself and wanted to go to the hospital. Several times we had to pull her back as she started out the front door. Finally we got her to lie down in the bedroom and she fell asleep.

Ruth and I poured glasses of lemonade for ourselves and sat out on the porch swing.

"Will they come home tonight?" I asked.

"I don't know. Depends."

We rocked in the darkness. I was suddenly exhausted.

I wanted to just slip down beside Ruth and go to sleep. This day had gone on forever.

Ruth's voice slipped through the darkness. "Your poor grandfather."

I sat up. "I guess he really was sick today."

I felt her stir beside me. "What do you mean?"

"Well, today, on the way to St. John's, he got very tired and had to rest a minute. I should have made him go home. Maybe this wouldn't have . . ."

"Annie, people don't often make your grandfather do things against his will. You know him well enough to know that." She paused. "Your mother told me about his visits to Timothy Lewis."

"She doesn't like him to go."

"I know. That's your mother."

"She doesn't want me to go, either."

"I didn't know you were visiting Timothy."

"I've been out twice with Grandfather. Oh, Ruth, you should have seen Mother today! We were all listening to Grandfather reading, Andrew had come back and it was all so peaceful and nice. She comes marching in, ignores Andrew and Timothy and orders Grandfather and me to leave. It was awful! And Andrew left. I know she hurt his feelings."

"Who is Andrew?"

"He's a patient out there. A friend of Timothy's." I paused. "And mine."

"How was he hurt?"

"He was burned. Father said he was probably gassed."

"Is it bad?"

"Yes, his face and hands."

"Did your mother tell you why she acted like that?"

"Yes. We had a big fight when we got home."

"What did she say?"

"That I wasn't to go out there, that Andrew was probably ashamed or upset about the way he looks and that he doesn't want visitors."

"Anything else?"

"That it would upset me because I'm just a child." I rocked harder, remembering the sting of Mother's words.

"Is she right?"

"What?"

"Is what she said true? Has this upset you . . . or him?"

"Well, yes, a little, at first. I didn't tell Mother this, Ruth, and promise you won't, but the first time I saw Andrew, I ran away."

"How did he act?"

"Well, he told me to leave."

"So your mother wasn't so wrong."

"Yes, but we've gotten used to each other. I can even look at him now and it doesn't make me feel . . . the way I did at first." For a moment, I couldn't believe I was admitting this, but it felt good. I went on. "We talked a little, and I think he would like me to come back. If Mother hasn't spoiled it all."

"Annie," Ruth said, reaching across to touch my arm, "your mother just wants to protect you, to let you be a child as long as possible. You've just run ahead of her and she doesn't realize it. She can't stand the thought of those men so she doesn't see how you can. She doesn't mean to be unfair or unkind."

We rocked steadily. Ruth's hand was warm on my arm.

"She said the war has hurt us enough."

"And it has. Do you have any idea what Paul meant to your mother?"

"I guess I never thought."

91

"Well, it's worth thinking about. Every one of those men could be her brother. They're still alive. And he isn't."

She said the last words softly and they slipped into the darkness around us.

So much to think about.

The swing lulled me and my eyelids drooped. Then I felt Ruth nudge me gently. "Come on, Annie. Let's get you inside. You can sleep on the couch until your parents get back."

I stumbled to the couch where I had seen my grandfather lying. I snuggled into its pillows and Ruth covered me with my grandmother's shawl. I had no time to even think of my grandfather before I slept.

12

I woke up the next morning in my own bed, and it was a moment before I remembered all that had happened the day before. I wondered how I'd gotten home. I lay in bed and listened to the silence of the house. No music from the piano, just the sun stretching across my bed. Then I remembered. I dressed hurriedly and rushed downstairs. Through the shadowed hall, I saw Ruth sitting on the front porch, reading the newspaper.

She looked up as I closed the screen. "Morning, sleepyhead."

"Hi. Where is everyone? Any news about Grandfather?"

"Everything's fine. He is doing much better. And your grandmother is at the hospital with your mother."

"Oh," I sighed. "For a minute, I thought . . ." Fidelio came out from under the bushes and stretched. I plunked down on the top step and he came to press against me. "When can I go see him?"

"That I don't know. Your mother said she'd be home in an hour or so. You can ask her then. How about some breakfast? Then I've got to be going. You'll be all right until she gets back?" Ruth paused on the doorstep and looked at me.

"Sure. I know you have to go. How do you put up with our family, anyway?" I had heard Father ask that many times about Ruth.

She grinned at me. "It's a challenge."

As long as I could remember, Ruth had been a part of my family's happy times and a reliable helper when we needed her. I had called her last night because I knew I wouldn't have to explain anything or anyone to her. If I told her we needed her, she would come.

"Thank you, Ruth, for talking to me last night. I'll think over what you said about Mother."

"Glad I could help, Annie." •

Emily arrived just as Ruth was leaving. She stood on the front porch, a large green bowl in her hands. When she saw me, she started to smile and then immediately looked serious.

"How are you, Annie? And how's your . . . Is he all right?"

"He's OK, Emily." I opened the door for her and she stepped in. "He'll be all right."

"Mama sent this over." She held out the bowl. "It's soup."

I tried to smile at her. Emily's mother made awful soup. "Thank you. Mother will really appreciate that. She's at the hospital with my grandmother."

"Oh."

"Come on. Do you want to see the new kittens?"

"I really can't stay very long. OK, just for a minute."

Over the new kittens, we forgot to be uncomfortable with each other. She told me about Bible School, how she and Darby read stories to the younger children and helped organize games and songs.

"The only thing wrong is that you're not there, Annie. I miss you."

I nodded.

"Aren't you sorry you decided not to come?"

I looked up at her. "No."

"Well, aren't you bored? What do you do all day?"

"Oh, things." I rolled a kitten over onto its back and tickled its tummy. "How did you find out about my grandfather?"

She forgot about my boredom as she listed the line of neighbors and friends who had passed the word about our troubles. By the time she left, we were talking the way we always had. As I closed the door behind her, I leaned against it for a moment and sighed. I was glad to have my friend back again. The only thing wrong was that I couldn't talk to her about all that was happening— my fight with Mother, the hospital, and Andrew.

Mother came home about noon. I heard the car stop across the street and then rumble down our driveway. I met her on the porch.

"How is he?"

"Let me catch my breath, Annie." She reached up and unwound the veil from around her face, took off her hat and sank onto a chair. She looked up at me. "Fine. He's fine for now. Don't worry." She reached out a hand to me and then put it to the high collar of her blouse and undid the top buttons. "It's beastly hot. And I'm exhausted."

I jumped up and ran to the icebox and poured Mother a tall glass of iced tea.

"Oh, thank you. Just the thing." She took two long gulps and then rested her head against the back of the swing. She did look exhausted. Her hair looped low about her face, her white blouse was wrinkled and limp.

I perched on the swing, the tips of my toes pushing me gently. I waited. I knew I had to give her a moment to catch her breath and then she'd tell me everything.

"Are you all right? What did you do all morning?" She didn't lift her head or open her eyes as she spoke.

"I'm fine. Emily was over. And guess what! She brought some of her mother's soup."

"Oh no," Mother groaned. Then she sighed. "I shouldn't say that. How nice of her, all the same. I'll call and thank her." She took another gulp of iced tea. "Well, your grandfather didn't have as bad an attack this time. But he's very weak."

I stopped swinging.

"He's sleeping now, is in no pain, and just needs to rest. But it's going to take him a little while to get over this. Thank goodness your father is here this time," she said as she reached up and smoothed back one lock of hair. "That makes it all bearable."

"When can I see him?"

"He'll be home tonight. He had to stop off at St. John's, but he'll be home—"

"No, I mean Grandfather. When can I see him?"

"Soon. He'll be home in a week or so. The doctors think he needs to get out of the heat for a while. That he needs a rest. You know yesterday he was up at five, out with his hens, then with you out to St. John's." She looked at me over her glass. "That kind of thing just wears him out. He's too old for that kind of nonsense."

I looked down at my lap. He doesn't think it's nonsense, I thought. And I don't either.

"So," she went on, "Grandmother and I have decided to take him out to Estes Park for a rest. As soon as he's well enough to travel, we'll go."

"Colorado?"

"Hmmm." She fanned herself with the newspaper Ruth had left on the chair. "You remember, that pretty cabin we had out in the woods. He can rest and walk there. Out of this miserable heat. Best thing for someone with a weak heart." She sat silent for a minute and then stood up. "Well, I have to take some lunch over to Mother. Maybe some soup." She smiled at me. And I hoped that meant a truce.

13

At first Mother said I must go with them to Colorado, that there was no question of my staying at home alone. "You will come with us," she said as she and Father rocked in the porch swing that evening. "Your father doesn't want to have to come home from work and take care of you."

She was treating me like a child again. If I did go to Colorado, I wouldn't be able to go out to St. John's for a long time. How could I persuade her?

Father put his arm around her. "Wait a minute, Katherine. How much taking care of does this big girl need? Besides, I'd rather like to have Annie here when I get home. I've missed seeing my girl for too long. I'm not sure I want to give her up anymore, even for a month or so."

I held my breath. Maybe Father would do the convincing for me.

"Oh, Lawrence, I don't know. What would you do all day, Annie?"

"I have a lot to do. I could read. Maybe work on math for next year. Besides, someone's got to take care of Grandfather's chickens and the cats. Oh, I'd love to stay."

Mother rocked for a few minutes. No one spoke. Finally, "Well, maybe you're right. I know I'll have my hands full. You would be of help, but I know you and your father need time together." She fanned herself, moving the sultry air around her face. "I will be glad to escape this heat, if only for a few weeks."

"See if you can't make your father stay longer. He needs to get all the fresh, cool air he can. And limit his walks to half an hour at first."

And their talk drifted into the details of the care my grandfather needed, mainly just rest and cool mountain breezes. After a while he even might go fishing, Father said. "If you can keep him there six weeks, through the hottest part of the summer, you'll do him a world of good."

Father and Uncle John brought Grandfather home a week later, the night before they were to leave. He was weakened and shaky, and changed in a way that frightened me just as it had after his first heart attack. After they helped him out of the car and up on the steps, he sat for a moment on the front porch, catching his breath before shuffling on into his bedroom. Grandmother skittered about him, moving furniture that wasn't in the way, pulling at the shawl that hung around his neck, repeating his name over and over. Father and Uncle John finally got him into the bedroom and settled. After a minute I tiptoed in to see him.

He lay stretched across the bed, a light quilt pulled up under his chin, rising, falling gently with his quiet breathing. One arm lay on the cover, the fingers curling up. I noticed his fingernails were clean. They usually had dirt under them from the rose bed or the vegetable garden.

Grandmother sat by his bed. A bitter medicine smell filled the room.

"Grandfather?" I touched his fingertips with mine.

"What? Hmmm? Oh, Annie, hello." Only his eyes moved. Then his fingers moved under mine.

"How are you feeling?"

"Oh, tired. This old man is tired. But it's good to be home."

Grandmother brushed his forehead with her hand.

"How's my best girl?"

"Fine, Grandfather."

"That's good. Sleepy now." He closed his eyes.

The next morning, our front hall stood crowded with bags and baskets, shawls for Grandmother and blankets for Grandfather. Father had joked that Mother was emptying the house. I wasn't going to the station, since Father and Uncle John were both going on to work after seeing them onto the train. I hugged Mother and Grandmother and then ran to the car where Grandfather already half sat, half lay.

"Grandfather," I whispered, "don't worry about Timothy. I'm going to see him and tell him where you've gone."

He patted my hand and winked at me. "That's my girl. I was hoping you would, but I was afraid to ask." He tipped his head to where Mother stood on the grass, tying her veil around her hair. "Listen, *Ivanhoe* is in the bookcase in the hall. You know the one. Do you think you could—"

I interrupted him. "Read to him? Sure."

"I have the page marked. Chapter Six, I think."

"I can't say all those French names very well."

Grandfather chuckled. "I can't either. Don't worry. I just back up and take a good running leap and usually manage to scramble over them." He patted my hand. "Besides, if you make a mess of it, who's to know?"

"Take care, Grandfather. Get strong. I'll miss you."

"You too, little love. Take care of your dad."

Last good-byes and then the two cars lumbered off, filled to the windows with luggage. I waved and stood looking down the empty street after they had disappeared around the corner. Suddenly the neighborhood was silent.

And I felt the silence inside of me. In the quiet, I heard Mother's last words to me. "Have a good time, Annie." She looked me in the eye. "Just remember our talk. I don't want you to go to St. John's again." I could still smell her powder and feel her veil on my cheek as she kissed me and hugged me to her.

I didn't go to St. John's that day. That night at dinner, Father and I talked about how far the train would have gotten. "They'll be traveling in style. You know your mother will see that they're comfortable."

"Were you comfortable when you came back from New York?"

"Not exactly. We were pretty crowded." He grinned at me. "But I knew I was coming home, and that made all the difference."

"Father," I said, not looking at him and rearranging the silverware on the table. "I'd like to go out to St. John's tomorrow to read to Timothy. I told Grandfather I would." I looked up at him. Had Mother talked to him?

"I don't see why not. I go pretty early, but you could come over later and spend the afternoon."

I could breathe again. Mother must not have had time to tell him about our argument. And she was out in western Kansas, near Fort Hayes by now, Father had said. He would never know, unless I told him. Was not telling him the same as lying? I had never lied to my parents. They were usually so reasonable that I had no need to. But now I did. And I hated it.

The next morning, I attended to all the chores at our house, the dishes, the beds, the animals. I cut some of Mother's roses and put them on the dining-room table. The house was quiet and cool.

I crossed the street and let myself in at my grandparents'. Uncle John had left his breakfast dishes in the sink, and I washed them and then went out back to feed the chickens. They rushed around my feet, gently clucking, ignoring Fidelio, who nosed them carefully.

Then I went to find *Ivanhoe*. It was nearing ten o'clock and I wanted to catch the ten-thirty streetcar. The book was right on the shelf where Grandfather had said it would be. Before I left, I peeked into the living room. The shades were drawn and already it smelled musty. Uncle John probably spent all his time in his room. In the shadows of the mantel, I could barely see Uncle Paul, his dark eyes looking out under the bill of his hat, his hands crossed in front of him. Beside the picture, his medals gleamed on the dark velvet. I stood silently a moment looking at my uncle's picture and then I turned and left. Timothy was waiting.

They were all outside when I got there, in their accustomed places under the trees. I wondered if they went outside as soon as the sun came up. Perhaps they escaped the hospital whenever they could.

I had to ask Sister Mary Frances where Timothy was, and it took us both a moment to find him. "He's been very sad since your grandfather fell ill. That dear man, I'm afraid he wasn't strong enough." The nun chattered to me as we walked among the men looking for Timothy. And Andrew. I was looking for him too.

We found Timothy sitting alone, his bandaged face tipped up as always, as if he spent his time listening to the air. Sister Mary Frances turned to me and smiled, then rustled away. She moved quietly, but Timothy turned and I sat down beside him.

"Hello, Timothy. It's Annie Metcalf. And I have *Ivanhoe*."

102

I read slowly that day, because Timothy had to explain all the characters to me, fill me in on the parts I had missed. I tried to "run" at the French names the way Grandfather had suggested, but I stumbled a lot. And we laughed a lot.

After about an hour, Timothy put a hand across the book and asked what time it was. "Time for my rest. They make me rest every day. You'll come back?"

I said I would and helped him into the hospital.

Before I left him, Timothy turned his face down to me. "You know Andrew Crayton? He came around the other day, asked if you'd been back. I told him about your grandfather. He's probably out somewhere. Maybe you could find him." I said I would.

14

The last time I had seen Andrew was the day Mother had come to the hospital. I knew he had seen the look on her face when she turned and looked at him. I wanted to tell him that I was not like her, that his face didn't frighten me anymore. But then I would have to admit to him how I had felt when I first saw his face. And I wasn't sure I could do that.

When I found him he was sitting alone under a tree. His first question was about my grandfather. When I told him they had gone to Colorado, he looked at me a moment and then asked, "Is that why you're here?"

I nodded. "Yes. Andrew, about my mother . . ."

"Never mind." He shook his head, his mouth pulled out of shape as it had been the first day. I sat down beside him.

"Too bad about your grandpa. Timothy sure misses him."

"Well, I'm going to take my grandfather's place. I mean, I'm going to read the book to him." I patted the heavy volume on my knee. "I'm doing it for my grandfather. He said Timothy had had enough disappointments."

Andrew looked down at his hands in their white bandages. "Timothy told me your uncle was killed in France."

"Yes, Uncle Paul." I paused. "He died last year."

"Where?"

"I'm not sure. A place with a name about trees. Or forests."

"Woods. Belleau Wood. That it?"

"Yes, it might be. Were you there?"

"No, we hadn't been brought up the line yet. My first battle was in the fall, in the Argonne. Another forest." He turned on the bench and brushed at his face with one bandaged hand.

"My uncle earned some medals for gallantry. So he must have been in the fighting a lot."

"Gallant under fire," Andrew muttered, "gallant under gas, gallant in the trenches while we kick 'em in the . . ." He stopped and shook his head. "Sorry. Just an old song."

"That's all right. I'm sure you were gallant too. Probably a hero." I looked at him, at the shadows on his face under his hat.

"Oh, yeah. I was a hero. A surefire hero." He laughed harshly and then coughed. After a moment, he went on. "I never did anything gallant." I looked up at him. His mouth twisted more than usual as he said, "It's hard to be very heroic in a foot of mud."

I didn't speak.

Then Andrew said, "Tell me about your uncle."

"He was handsome." I thought of him in the dark cape lined with red, smiling as he told me good night. "Tall, and he wore a little mustache. He loved music, like my mother." I stopped a moment. "He was her brother."

"You must miss him."

For a moment I could only nod. Then I said, "He made me feel I was important. He listened to me." I thought of our talk that night at the opera, when he had told me I was wise.

"Don't other people listen to you?"

"Oh, yes, Mother and Father do. Usually. But Uncle Paul was different. He didn't *have* to pay attention to me, but he did. And that made me feel . . ." I tried to find the word and finally just shrugged. "That made me feel as if I was important to him."

Andrew nodded slowly. "That makes sense. Go on."

So I told him about the day Frederick McFarland, my uncle's friend, came to tell us how he died. I had been out in the yard with Grandfather feeding the hens and jumping mudholes when a car, bigger than our car and shiny, drove in the driveway and parked by the house. But no one got out. Grandfather and I looked at each other. Then he picked his way across the muddy, hen-soaked yard to the car. I watched as a young man in a clean khaki uniform got out and shook Grandfather's hand. They talked a moment and then Grandfather shook his hand again and led him around to the back door. He called out to my grandmother as they stood on the porch scraping mud off their boots, and then they both went into the kitchen.

All I could hear was the gurgling of the melting snow trickling under the hen house and down into the creek below. I stood for a moment in the sun, wondering if I should go home or go inside. Grandfather seemed to have forgotten me. I emptied my bowl of chickfeed on the high ground under the maple tree and sloshed back to the house, leaving the smell of mud and the pale warmth of the winter sun to the hens and to Fidelio, who was asleep on top of Grandfather's tool shed.

The kitchen was empty, so I tiptoed down the long hall to the living room. My grandparents were sitting together on the high-backed couch and Grandmother was crying. The young man sat across the room from them, his uniform cap in his lap. I knew that this stranger was talking about Uncle Paul.

"Annie, come meet Lieutenant Frederick McFarland. He was a friend to Paul." As I shook his hand, I wondered if he had seen my uncle die. He smiled at me.

"I'm pleased to meet you, Annie." He half stood as he shook my hand.

"Go on." My grandfather reached to take my grandmother's hand.

"Well, as I was saying, sir, the Second Division had been sent up to relieve the Marines who'd been in battle for four days. It was fierce fighting and the losses were . . . heavy." He moved a bit in his seat and crossed his legs. "We were in a large wooded area, an old hunting preserve, we heard, that was covered with trees and huge boulders. A bad spot for a fight. It was there that your son died." He paused and cleared his throat.

"Were you with him?"

The soldier swallowed. "No, sir. But he died a hero, I know."

"How do you know?"

"Because he was a leader, a real leader, I mean, who always thought of his men, and I know that he probably died trying to help one of them."

That seemed to satisfy my grandfather. He sat back and nodded. Grandmother continued to cry.

"You should be very proud of your son." The soldier was still talking. "He was a brave man."

I knew Uncle Paul had done something brave before he died. He would have risked his life gladly, laughing as he had on the motorcycle. And this soldier had said he was a leader. I could picture him surrounded by his men, showing them the battle map, or encouraging them when they were afraid.

Grandfather blew his nose. "This is all good to know. We only had the letter before from his commanding officer. And, of course, the telegram."

"Yes, well, they asked me to come out on my way home

and answer any questions you might have. And to reassure you that your son didn't suffer." He swallowed again and then took out a handkerchief and wiped his face. Then he drank his tea, refused a slice of Grandmother's Christmas cake and left. He never came back, even though Grandfather asked him to stay in touch. But he had talked about the place where Paul died, in the forest that Andrew called Belleau Wood.

Andrew sat silent when I finished.

"How do you spell the name of the forest where my uncle died?"

"Not forest. Wood. Belleau Wood. B-e-l-l-e-a-u. It's French. Someone told me it means pretty water."

"So my uncle died in the woods by the pretty water."

"Something like that." Suddenly he reached behind me to the table we leaned against. "That's why they gave him one of these." And he tossed a small box onto my lap. His name was written across the top. "Go ahead. Open it."

I looked at him again to be sure he wanted me to open the box. He was looking up into the shaded afternoon.

I opened the box carefully and saw a medal lying upside down in the box as if thrown there. As I lifted it out, it untangled itself and swung from my hand. A ribbon and a purple heart so dark it looked black hung from a bar covered in purple silk. On the heart was the profile of George Washington.

"It's so beautiful. What is it?" I reached out and touched the heart. Smooth and cool.

"The Purple Heart."

"What?"

"Purple Heart. Don't you know about it? Your uncle must have one. They hand them out like penny candy.

Everybody here has one, that's for sure." Andrew's voice was too loud as he got up, shoving his hand into his pocket. "Some general came around today and gave them out to all the guys in my unit. They must have brought a wagonload."

I looked at the little heart, black against the palm of my hand. "Why did they give it to you?"

"Like I said, I was a hero. A dumb, surefire hero." He croaked out each word in his hoarse, pain-filled voice. Then he stopped and held one hand to his eyes and I saw his hand was shaking. When he spoke again, his voice was softer. "They give these to anyone wounded or killed in battle. Everyone has one practically. Or their families do."

"I don't think Uncle Paul got one. Grandmother has his medals in a case, all laid out on velvet. I'll check." I laid the ribbon carefully in the box, the heart faceup. "It's beautiful." I tried to imagine how Uncle Paul would have looked if he had lived to wear all his medals, how they would have looked pinned on his khaki jacket.

"I could do without it." Andrew turned away abruptly.

I stared at his back a moment and then got up from the table and walked back along the path, leaving him alone. As I walked through the shadows, I looked at every soldier, wanting to see Uncle Paul. He was there, standing just beyond the corner of my eye, and if I turned suddenly, I thought, I might see him, watching me, his head cocked and the half smile brightening his serious face.

Late in the afternoon, when Father came to take me home, I was sitting again with Andrew under the trees. He said hello to Andrew and asked how he was feeling.

"Oh, just great. Fine and dandy."

Father put both hands in his jacket pockets and looked down at Andrew. He didn't smile, and Andrew sighed and said, "Sorry. I'm OK."

"How's that one tender spot?"

Andrew's hand went to his mouth again. "Still hurts. Especially when I eat."

"We may still have to do more with that then. We'll try more therapy first. Don't worry, Andrew. You may not need more surgery. We'll see."

I looked at Andrew's mouth. All of his skin looked tender and sore. How could one spot be worse than all the rest? I wanted to ask about it, but Father turned away.

"Let's go, Annie. See you tomorrow, Andrew."

I said good-bye to Andrew and he waved without looking at me. He still seemed to be far away. Maybe he too was looking out under the trees, to the far-distant woods, where handsome men and boys with dark eyes fought and died.

15

After dinner that evening, I went to my grandparents' house to look at Paul's medals again. I had never paid much attention to them before, not listened when Grandfather had talked about what each one meant. I thought I would have noticed the beautiful Purple Heart if it had been there, but I wanted to be sure. I turned on the light in the shadowy living room and then carefully took down the heavy oak frame from the mantel where it sat beside the picture of Uncle Paul. I smoothed the velvet as it lay on my lap. At the top was a star hanging from a red ribbon. Three round medals lay in a row beneath the star. At the bottom were several gold bars and a white cloth star with an Indian head on it. I remember Grandfather saying this was the symbol of Paul's division. The bars were lieutenant bars. The others above must be medals, the ones he had earned for gallantry.

But no Purple Heart. Maybe Grandfather had put that one away, thinking it would upset Grandmother too much to look at it. Father wouldn't know, since he hadn't been here when the box of Uncle Paul's belongings had arrived. I had watched as Grandfather and Mother unwrapped the package: his shaving kit, a book of poems by William Carlos Williams, his pistol, and the medals. They found three letters in the book, one from me and two from Grandmother. They also found a picture of a girl. She was wearing a white fur hat tipped to one side to show her dark hair waving over one eye. She had a tiny nose and a wide, happy smile. And no freckles. I looked at the picture a long time before I left it facedown on Grandmother's table. Grandmother let me take my letter and the book of poems.

After they had looked through the package, Grandfather and Mother put all of Uncle Paul's things back in the box and decided that Grandmother could see all of it. I wondered what they wouldn't have let her see.

Grandfather would know if among the medals was a Purple Heart. I would have to write and ask him. Uncle Paul should have every medal he deserved and if a mistake had been made, we needed to find out. After all, he had been a hero.

I sat down that evening to write. I first wrote a careful letter to Mother, describing in detail my care of the two houses and what Father and I had talked about in the evening and how much fun it was to be on my own. It was hard to fill up the letter without mentioning St. John's, but I knew I would have to write such letters as long as Mother was away. I didn't like hiding things from her, but her unreasonable attitude made this necessary.

Then I wrote a cheery note to Grandfather and just slipped in a question about the medal at the end in case Mother read the letter. I knew it would be several weeks before I could expect a reply. It was going to be hard to wait patiently to find out about the medal. But I could wait. I had to know.

I went to St. John's every day for the next week. We moved quickly through *Ivanhoe* and I became as engrossed in the story as Timothy was. Several mornings Andrew came to sit under a tree and listen, but not every day. Timothy always seemed glad to have him there, and by the way they talked to each other I could tell they spent a lot of time together. They talked about the other men—who was improving, who'd had an operation, who was going home. Once or twice they mentioned men who had died. They never talked about the war or complained in front of me.

Even though I'd gotten used to Andrew's anger, I still hated those moments when his mouth drooped and he turned away from me. I knew I shouldn't let it bother me, especially after Timothy told me that Andrew was always more cheerful when I was around. But I still was afraid of his bitterness.

I told him about my letter to Grandfather and how I couldn't wait for a reply.

"It's really that important to you?"

"Yes, why not?"

"Medals . . ." He shrugged. "They won't bring him back."

"I know that."

"Just so long as you remember that. They're just metal and ribbon."

In the afternoons, Andrew and I often played checkers. I had learned to play with Grandfather, but I had to struggle to beat Andrew. And he never just let me win. Other days when he was having therapy, I sat under the trees and looked at my books. Occasionally, one of the patients would call me by name and I realized they were beginning to accept having me there. The nuns asked me to run errands, to deliver letters and messages. I loved helping them because they always were so busy and were grateful for my help. Andrew began to tease me.

"We'll have to get you a white veil and a red cross," he said. "You're getting to be a regular Florence Nightingale."

I laughed, but I had to admit to myself that I liked to

imagine wearing the crisp white clothes and graceful veils of the nurses I saw in the newspapers. One afternoon I imagined a whole story, that I had run away from home to join the nurse corps and that my mother had disowned me. I was in a hospital in France near the front lines and one day Paul was brought in, near death. He recognized me and said he could now die happy because I was there. I helped him write a letter to Mother in which he begged her to forgive me. Then he died, holding my hand.

The sun had moved through the afternoon and I was no longer in the shade. It was really hot. I took off my hat and fanned myself.

Footsteps. I looked behind me and saw Andrew coming off the grassy slope toward me. His hat covered his face in the shadows. His white bandages almost blinded me, glaring in the sun.

"Andrew, hello."

He waved one white hand. "Hi, Annie. Let's find a bench under the trees. It's a hot one." He looked down at me as we climbed the slope, me lugging my bookbag. "Always the bag. What happens if you're caught without it?"

"You wait. I made cookies last night."

He seemed in a good mood. He hadn't been around that morning and I wondered where he had been, but I didn't want to upset him by asking. We stood in the shade and looked into the cool cave under the trees, peopled again by the quiet solemn men. Andrew paid no attention to them but guided me to a wooden table.

After we sat down, he held up his right hand. The bandages were gone from his fingers. "Look. The doctors say it won't be long until my whole hand's free."

"That's wonderful. Aren't you happy?"

114

As he looked at me, a corner of his mouth twitched and I instantly realized that I had said the wrong thing. He gave a harsh laugh. "Happy?" His lips tightened and he shrugged and turned away, leaning on his arm.

We sat in silence, the checkerboard between us. He took off his hat and brushed the hair off his forehead where it clung in brown curls. In the dark light of the shadows, his face looked less hot and angry, the color faded. Shadows clustered around his eyes. He didn't seem to be in a hurry to start the game. We didn't move as minutes passed.

Suddenly: "How can you stand to look at me?" Andrew spoke quietly, almost whispering.

For a moment, I couldn't speak. Then I said, "Andrew, I . . . I've gotten used to it, I guess. It's not so bad."

He shook his head, eyes closed. "Yes, it is." Then he put his hand to his mouth, as he did so often.

"Does your face hurt?"

Andrew opened his eyes and smoothed the bookbag with his hand. "Not much now. But at first. Oh, God, it hurt so bad, I wanted to die."

He rested his forehead on his hand. "And every time I look in the mirror now, I want to die." He looked down at the table. "Or when I catch people looking at me out of the corners of their eyes."

He brought both hands to his mouth and closed his eyes for a moment.

"You're the only one, besides the sisters here and the other fellows, you're the only civilian, so to speak, who's ever really looked at me straight on, without turning away. Like you're doing now. Like you did that day when you first saw me. Just looked me in the face."

I looked down at the bookbag. But I had turned away, I thought. Turned and run away.

115

"You're just a girl, but you're the first to treat me like I wasn't terrible."

He suddenly stood up and leaned against the trunk of the huge tree that sheltered us. "OK with you if I smoke? I can manage it, now my fingers are free." He paused, his hand inside the pocket of his robe.

I nodded quickly and then watched as he awkwardly tapped out a cigarette, lighted it and blew out the smoke. It curled around his face and then melted in the hot air.

"Maybe a kid like you shouldn't hang around a mess like me." He watched me through the smoke. "Maybe I'm giving you nightmares."

I shook my head. "No, Andrew, I promise. You don't upset me. Except that I worry that you're in pain."

He sat down across from me again.

"My mother said the same thing—that I shouldn't come anymore," I said.

"She did, huh? I didn't think she liked me much." He took a deep breath of the cigarette and blew it high into the air between us. "So why are you here?"

"Well, I'm old enough to decide things for myself. Things that are important."

"And your mom's not home now, right?"

I had been busy buckling and unbuckling the straps of the bookbag as he said this. Now I looked up into Andrew's face. He was grinning, his mouth pulled back from his teeth. I nodded, but I couldn't help smiling a little.

"Well, if that don't beat the band," he said.

"My father thinks it's all right. And he'll talk to Mother when she gets home. He'll convince her."

"I sure hope so. I do look forward to seeing you." He had never said before that he was glad to see me, not to my face. And because he had said that, I had the courage

116

to ask what I suddenly realized I wanted to know.

"Andrew, what happened to you?"

He pushed a black checker piece around the board. "Why do you want to know? Because of your uncle?"

I shook my head. No, that wasn't why I asked.

He looked at me, frowning, brown eyes worried. "I probably shouldn't tell you. Give you nightmares. Your mom's right." Then he shifted and turned sideways so all I could see was the side of his face. He leaned on his elbow, the newly uncovered hand resting on the table between us.

"Everyone used gas—we did, the Germans did. Different kinds did different things, all pretty awful. I got it from mustard gas—Yellow Cross, we called it."

I nodded. I didn't dare ask questions for fear he would stop talking.

Then he turned back to face me. He set the checkers in two rows, facing black to red. "The trenches lay out like this across the fields. Used to be farmers' fields, but by the time we saw them, they were ruined. Probably never be good again. So much poison . . . Anyway, we lived inside the trenches, like earthworms hiding from robins." A brief smile on his face. "We crept along in them, often in mud up to the tops of our boots. We ate, we slept, sometimes we fought, we wrote our letters home inside those trenches. But then, in the big battle, it got worse. The gas came."

He stopped and I waited.

"It kept low to the ground, like fog. It looked like fog except it was yellow and it smelled bad. It would stay in holes in the ground, you know, shell holes and the like. That's how some of the guys got it, when they jumped in shell craters to get away from bullets and the gas got 'em instead. I got it because I lost my gas mask. We were going through some bushes, high straggly stuff in the Argonne Forest. I kept it hooked on my belt instead of around my neck like they told us to do." He stopped a minute. "It must have gotten snagged on something. With all that was going on, I didn't notice it was gone until we heard the whistle of gas shells and then that smell. I went for my mask and it wasn't there. Nothing I could do."

"Did it burn?"

"Not at first. It took a while. They told us to wash all over and change clothes if we took gas. Real easy to do in the middle of a battle." He pushed the checkers to one side. "That afternoon I knew I was in trouble, and they sent me back to the brigade hospital in an artillery wagon. No ambulances. But the shelling was so bad, the horses spooked and we had to stop. We spent the night in a bombed-out school. By the time I got to the hospital, the pain was so bad I would have shot myself if I'd still had my gun."

I'd seen pictures of soldiers in the gas masks that made them look like ugly fish. Uncle Paul had mentioned gas in a joking way in one of his letters, saying it had convinced him to stop smoking. I'd never thought it was like this.

"Anyway, that taught me not to lose things." I looked up at Andrew and he reached out one hand, but didn't touch me. "That's enough. I got out alive. A lot didn't."

He began to set up the checker pieces, moving slowly with his half-free hand. "Let's have a game." The skin on that hand was bright pink, like his face, and scarred. I thought of how he must have put his hands to his face when he smelled the gas. And how badly his hands and face must have hurt. At least Uncle Paul had died quickly, without such pain.

I'd brought a book about Egypt, so after the game we read the captions and examined the photographs of pyramids and statues. I told him about my dream of sailing up the Nile, and about Ruth. I asked him if he would like to see Egypt and he said he would.

Father came to collect me about five. The sun had fallen low behind the hospital and most of the men had already gone inside for dinner. I walked Andrew to the door of the hospital and watched until he disappeared down the long, dim corridor. My hand still tingled from the last squeeze he had given it.

16

Dear Annie,

What a treat to come home from our walk and find a letter from my best girl. Sounds like you and your dad are having a grand time together. I hope the old hens aren't giving you trouble. Just tell 'em I'll make stew out of them when I get back if they're bad.

We're enjoying the mountains and the fresh air. The cabins are as comfortable as ever and the Jacobsens are fine hosts. I'm eating more than is good for me, I know. But I feel fine, good as new. Tell your dad not to worry about me. My guess is we'll be home quick as a train. Don't be surprised to see us.

Yesterday, I fed some ground squirrels from our back porch. Made me think of you and how much you'd enjoy all the animals around here. We see deer every evening and sometimes on our afternoon walks. No moose yet. We'll have to plan a trip out here together—soon.

About Paul's medals. You're right, he probably should have a Purple Heart. I never thought about that before, but then I don't put much store by the ribbons, seeing what they replaced. It's your grandmother who does. Anyway, there was no Purple Heart among the medals the army sent us. Must be a slipup somehow. If you want to show your dad the telegram we got after Paul's death, it's in the big Bible somewhere in the front room. I'm not sure where your grandmother last put it. I'm quite sure the telegram is still there. Your dad might want to see it.

I can't wait to see you. It sure is pleasant here, but it's not home. Take care of your dad. See you soon.

Love,
Grandfather

"Why, he sounds fine," Father said when I showed him the letter. "I bet he is anxious to get home. Your grandfather isn't one to sit around." Then he looked at me through the air from his fragrant pipe. "What's this about Paul's medals, Annie? I didn't know you were a medal expert."

"I'm not. Andrew just got his Purple Heart. And I wondered why Uncle Paul hadn't been given one."

"It's only given for battle-related wounds or death."

"But Uncle Paul died in battle, at Belleau Wood."

Father nodded. "Yes, he did from all accounts. Sounds a bit odd." He smiled at me. "Miss Sherlock Holmes."

"Don't laugh at me, Father. I just think that Uncle Paul should have all the glory he deserves, all the medals he can get. Don't you?"

He looked at me a moment without saying anything. Then he said, "How does Andrew feel about his medal?"

I remembered his words and the way he'd thrown the little box with the beautiful medal onto the table. "He said he could do without it."

Father puffed his pipe a moment and looked out over the evening-cool yard. "Hmmm."

"But anyway, I still think Uncle Paul should have it."

"I agree. Or we should find out why he doesn't have one." He got up and tapped his pipe out over the edge of the porch onto the dirt. "Shall we go over and scout out that telegram? Might tell us something."

"Oh, can we? Right now?"

"After you, my dear Holmes."

We found the telegram in the Bible, just as Grandfather had said. Father unfolded it, moved to the front window and read the paper silently. Then he looked up at me.

"You've read this before? When it first came?"

I nodded. "But I don't remember what it says."

He turned back to the paper in his hand. "Not much here." Then he read it aloud.

Dear Mr. and Mrs. MacLeod:

I regret to inform you that your son, 1st Lieutenant Paul MacLeod, died in the service of his country in France on June 6, 1918. Please accept my deepest sympathies.

Newton Baker
Secretary of War

Father's hand dropped to his side and he looked at me.

"That's all? I thought it was longer."

He turned the telegram over. "No, that's all." He handed it to me. And I read it again.

"It doesn't say how he died."

"No, it doesn't. And all that anyone knows is what Lieutenant McFarland told your grandparents?"

"And he didn't say much, except that Uncle Paul died like a hero."

Father looked back at the telegram. "I wonder . . ." He paused. "Well"—folding the telegram—"doesn't really matter how he died, I guess."

"But what about the Purple Heart?"

Father gently laid the telegram back in the Bible and closed the covers. "Yes, the Purple Heart. Annie, Paul just may not get one. Is it so important?"

I looked at his picture on the mantel, the black ribbon stretched taut across it. My handsome uncle, his dark hair smooth, his eyes serious, the collar of his uniform high under his chin.

Did it matter how he died? And was a medal so important?

I'd planned to tell Andrew about Grandfather's letter the next day but, when I found him, he wasn't alone. He lounged on the grass beside a woman sitting in a wicker chair. I stopped when I saw her and was about to turn away when Andrew stood up and waved to me.

"Annie!"

I stepped onto the grass and walked toward them. Andrew looked different, and it took me a minute to realize that he wasn't in his usual bathrobe and pajamas but was dressed in pants and a loose green shirt. He didn't look the same at all. I felt nervous, as if I was meeting two strangers instead of one.

"Annie, come and meet my mother." She smiled up at me and said hello. While I waited for Andrew to find a chair for me, I looked at Mrs. Crayton. She sat, hands folded in her lap, as if she were waiting in a doctor's office. Her hair was lighter than Andrew's and pulled back in a low bun. She looked older than my mother, her skin rough-looking, her plain dark dress covering her shoes. Her eyes were warm, the color of earth, just like Andrew's.

"Andrew says you've been a real friend to him," Mrs. Crayton said. "That's real nice of you." She reached out and put her hand on Andrew's arm. "And your dad is a doctor here?"

I nodded.

"Will he be doing your operation, dear?"

"No, Mom. I told you." Andrew frowned at her.

"Oh." She put a hand to her mouth. "I'm sorry. I guess I wasn't supposed to say anything. I'm sorry."

"That's OK." He got up and leaned against a tree. "She'd

know, sooner or later. I'm having another operation day after tomorrow, Annie."

"Oh. Why . . . I mean, I didn't know you were still having . . . ?"

"I'll probably have more surgery for years to come. Until they've gotten tired of looking at my ugly face. I know I already am." He reached into the pocket of his shirt. "Oh, damn, I don't have . . . I'll be right back." And he walked up the path to the hospital.

His mother sighed. "Cigarettes, I suppose. He always smokes more when he's unhappy. Andrew used to be a happy boy. Always helpful and ready to get up and do. He's so changed. Like a different person, almost. I think this operation really has upset him. I don't think he expected it." She leaned toward me. "He called me and asked me to come out early. I don't usually come until Saturday. But he wanted me to come before the operation."

She reminded me a little of my grandmother, the way she chattered on without stopping.

She smoothed her dress over her knees. I noticed how red her hands were. "I wish I could be here for him more. That's why it's nice he has you for a friend. He talks about you a lot."

I felt myself blush. "Where do you live?"

"Out in Stull. Our place is about five miles out of town." Stull was a tiny town west of Kansas City where we had gone once on a school picnic to visit the old cemetery.

"It must be fun to live on a farm."

"Oh, I'd not call it fun. It's so much hard work. That's why . . . " She stopped talking and looked over her shoulder toward the hospital. Wisps of her faded brown hair had come loose from the knot at the back of her head and waved around her face. Her hair looked fine, like mine. I reached up and smoothed my own hair back from my face.

"No, a farm is a lot of hard work. We're real busy. So we don't get in much." She picked up her purse and took out a handkerchief and wiped her forehead.

"Didn't your husband come in with you?"

She looked across at me, frowning a little. "Does Andrew talk about his dad ever?"

I shook my head. I didn't tell her that he had never talked about any of his family.

"Well"—she sighed—"I guess he wouldn't mind. Andrew's dad is out on the street. Sitting in the truck."

I turned and looked out into the sun. "Why? It's hot out there."

"Because he won't come in and see Andrew. He hasn't seen his son since the day the boy went off to the army."

"Why not?"

"Because he blames Andrew for what happened to him in France. Says he didn't have to go."

"It's not Andrew's fault! That's not fair!" I exploded.

"You probably don't remember back when the war started, Annie, or when they started taking men into the army."

"Yes, I do." I thought of Uncle Paul and his friends in their stiff new uniforms. "I remember the parades down Baltimore Avenue."

"Well, we didn't have any parades in Stull. But Andrew and his pals got excited anyhow. Said they wanted to enlist. You see, they didn't draft farmers or their sons, since they needed food for the army. So Andrew could have stayed home and been safe." She suddenly put her handkerchief to her mouth. She took a deep breath. "He could have been safe. But he went. I guess seeing France was too big a chance for a boy who'd lived all his life on the farm."

I suddenly realized I had been gripping the sides of the wicker chair. I let go and felt where the ridges of the chair had dug into my palms. He didn't have to go. He hadn't been drafted. He had wanted to go. Just like Uncle Paul.

Mrs. Crayton sighed. "Anyway, his father has never forgiven him. Even when Andrew was hurt. His father never said anything about that, even though they'd been close before. He won't come to see Andrew. He drives me here but won't set foot inside the hospital."

I stared at her. What did Andrew's father have to forgive? This didn't make sense.

"Now promise me, Annie, you won't tell Andrew I told you. He's very proud and wouldn't want you to know. I probably shouldn't have. But it helps to talk about it."

I swallowed and then promised. No wonder Andrew never talked about his family.

Then she asked about my family and soon I was talking about my grandparents, Mother's music, school, usual normal things. I didn't realize how long we'd been talking until Mrs. Crayton looked out at the sun.

"Where did that boy go? I'll have to leave soon."

"I'll go see." I started to get up when I saw Andrew coming down the path with Timothy. "Here he comes."

"Look who I found hiding in a corner. Had to drag him out here." Andrew guided Timothy to a bench and then lightly punched his arm. "Tell them. Tell them the news."

Timothy tipped his head back like he always did and smiled, a wide, happy look on his face. "They're coming off. My bandages are coming off."

I clapped my hands. "When? When?"

"A week or so. The doctors just decided today after they checked me again."

"What grand news, Timothy." Mrs. Crayton got out of her chair and leaned over and kissed him on the cheek, below his bandages. "I'm so happy for you."

He reached out a hand to her and she took it. I realized then that they knew each other, that they must have met on one of her visits.

He turned his face in my direction. "You write and tell your grandfather that he'd better hurry home or I'll finish *Ivanhoe* myself."

We all laughed, and suddenly I felt that I wanted to laugh and cry and sing all at the same moment. I think I might have gotten up and hugged Timothy and Andrew and his mother if she hadn't said just then that she had to go.

She and Andrew started down the path together. They walked to the turn in the path and then I saw her reach up and kiss him on the cheek. She loved him enough not to mind that his face was rough and scarred. But his father wouldn't even speak to him. I wondered what Mr. Crayton would do if Andrew one day walked up to the truck and said hello. I wanted to be there if it ever happened.

But not today. Andrew only stood on the shady path, looking after his mother as she walked away. I didn't want him to know I had been watching him, so I went back to sit with Timothy. He was where we'd left him, his head cocked in that curious, listening way. He was still smiling.

17

I didn't go to the hospital the next morning because Father said Andrew would be having tests to get him ready for surgery. At noon Father called to say he'd take me out after dinner to see Andrew. He said he had to go back anyway. One of his patients was dying.

Father always took the motorcycle to St. John's, and I'd gotten used to riding behind him. While no ride was ever like that first one with Uncle Paul, I always enjoyed it, the wind, the speed. But now as I hung on to the back of the motorcycle I shivered. I didn't know if the air was cooler than usual or if it was going out at night and my concern over Andrew that made goose bumps come all over my arms. Father parked the motorcycle on the path by the steps to the front door. The grass under the trees looked empty, dark and silent.

"I'll tell Andrew you're here. You can't come inside this late in the evening. Where will you be?"

"Over on the bench. On the other side." I pointed to the bench where we had first met, the bench that was usually too sunny but that tonight faced out over a field of shadows and moonlight.

"I'll try not to be too long. Andrew needs to rest too." And Father paused a moment and looked at the lights of the hospital. Inside, his patient was dying. I wondered who it was.

I waited on the bench, shivering a little as the wet air settled around me. The light from the tall windows stretched out on the lawn to the left of me and I could hear music from Victrolas and from the piano in the dining room. Occasionally I heard laughter.

Then Andrew was there, slipping so quietly onto the bench that I only knew he had come by the smell of the strong hospital soap.

"Hiya, Annie."

"Hello, Andrew. How are you?"

"Well, not awfully good. Had kind of a bad day."

In the moonlight I could see the bandage on his left hand still wrapped high on his arm. He flexed his right hand. The doctors had taken off more bandages, almost to his elbow.

"I got a letter back from my grandfather." I spoke more to get his mind off the operation than anything.

"Oh?" He looked over at me. "Any news about the medal?"

"No. Grandfather didn't know anything about it." We sat in silence a moment. "Father and I read the telegram they sent when he died."

"Oh, yeah. We always heard about those. What did it say?"

I told him. He listened and then said, "June sixth? Is that what it said?"

"Yes. Why?"

"I'm not sure. Probably nothing."

"Andrew, I get the feeling something is strange about all this. Am I right?"

"I don't know. Let me think about it and ask around. Don't worry. There's plenty of time."

Time for what? I wondered.

All of a sudden, Andrew shivered beside me. "I'm getting a bit damp out here. You must be too. Come wait for your dad inside." We got up and walked toward the hospital.

"I'll wait on the steps. Father said not to come inside." I stopped.

Andrew let out a low whistle, more of a hiss than anything. "Oh, boy. Look at that." He was looking at the motorcycle. "I've heard about the motorcycle your dad rides. Did you come on that tonight?"

"Yes. It was my uncle's. I rode it once with him." I touched the handlebars that shone in the bright night.

He stood and looked at it a moment without speaking. Then he said, so low I almost didn't hear him, "What I wouldn't give . . ." He knelt by the motorcycle and ran his good hand along the length of the gleaming pipes. He put his hands on the handlebars, but the bandaged one wouldn't quite curl around it. He lifted his hands and stepped back. "It's fine. Real fine."

"Maybe my father would let you ride it."

"Yeah, sure—with these." He lifted his bandaged hand. "You need *two* good hands to do most things, remember?"

"But your one hand got better. The other one will too. Don't give up hope."

"Oh, I know, Annie. It's just hard to be patient." Then he shivered. "I better get back inside. They'll be hunting me down. What's your dad doing inside this late?"

"He said someone was dying."

Andrew tipped his head back and looked at the sky.

"Someone is dying," he repeated. Then he reached down for my hand. "Did he ever tell you that we're all dying?"

"Andrew," I said softly and I put my hand on his arm.

For one moment, I felt him touch the top of my head as he kissed my hair.

As we rode home through the silent city, I could still feel that gentle pressure. Andrew had kissed me. I felt the way I did after my night ride with Uncle Paul, as if I knew a secret that made the world wonderful.

I couldn't tell Father what had happened, but suddenly I wanted to talk to him about Andrew. So I told him what Mrs. Crayton had told me about Andrew enlisting and about his father.

"Oh, that's too bad." Father put his arm around me as we walked toward the house from the garage. "Just makes it all the rougher for him, doesn't it?"

I nodded, afraid that if I began to speak, I might say too much. I let Fidelio out and went in to put on a light. When I came out, Father was standing looking out into the dark. I sat on the swing and rubbed Fidelio's ears and looked at Father where he stood without moving.

"Father, what's wrong?"

He turned to look at me and smiled quickly. "Nothing, Annie. I'm just . . ." He brushed his hair with his hand. Then he shook his head. "I'm just tired, I guess. And I miss your mother." He came and sat beside me. We rocked slowly. "We'll have to go in in a minute." But neither of us moved.

"What kind of surgery is Andrew having?"

"Nothing serious. Just another try at rebuilding his mouth, at repairing the damage and removing some of the scar tissue."

"Will he have a lot more pain?"

"I don't know. Hard to say. Probably not a lot more."

I hadn't meant to say what I did, I hadn't planned it. Father seemed so tired and sad himself. But suddenly I was angry.

131

"Why did you tell me last spring that the worst was over for the men you treated, that they were happy to be home? And that they didn't hurt anymore? Why did you tell me all that?"

Father looked at me, frowning. "When did I say that?"

"Right after you came home. When I asked you about the men at the train station."

Father turned to look at me, frowning. "I don't remember. But you must be right. You always did have a superb memory."

"You *knew* that was a lie! Why did you say those things to me? You couldn't have believed what you said." I was almost shouting.

"Annie, calm down. No. How could I say that they didn't hurt anymore when for some of them every day is absolute hell?"

"But you said it."

"I was a fool to tell you such nonsense. I guess . . . I wanted to protect you somehow from all that I had seen. When I left for the war, you were still a child. You grew up while I was away." Father brushed his face with his hand. "Maybe for Andrew the worst is past. But he definitely still has pain. And as to being happy, well, maybe he is or can be, but many of the others . . ." Father stopped.

We sat without speaking, side by side on the swing, night sounds surrounding us. Then Father leaned forward, elbows on his knees. I looked at the back of his head, the back and shoulders I had known all my life. I thought to myself that a stranger sat beside me, someone I didn't know at all.

"Father," I began. He sat back and I went on. "I wanted to believe you. I didn't want to know how awful life was for those men I saw the day you came home. I think I just

132

wanted to think that everyone went off and died the way Uncle Paul did, quickly and neatly. So I let you lie to me."

Father pulled back from me on the swing. "I haven't been a very good father to you, Annie. I haven't helped you as I should. I'm having trouble with all of this myself, to be quite honest. Seeing all these . . . seeing how little there is I can do. Maybe your mother is right. Maybe we should just let it all go. Just forget."

"No, no, *no!* How can you say that? Listen, they are getting better. Andrew is better, isn't he? He's got the bandages half off one hand and soon off the other. And look at Timothy! Why, he'll be able to see in a little while. *See!* Just think of that. There is a lot you're doing. Oh, don't give up and be discouraged. Someone has got to keep caring about those men."

The swing was swaying in wild jerks as I pounded on the arm. Suddenly I realized Father was laughing, first silently and then out loud.

"Oh, Annie, you're good for the soul. I'm so glad you're here. I need you to keep me cheerful. And honest."

"Well, it's all true."

"Of course it is. We do have much to be thankful about. So much."

"I think so."

"You're right. Now, how about some of that ice cream Aunt Felicia brought over this evening?"

Before he left the next morning, Father told me he would phone as soon as he knew anything about Andrew's condition. "And it'll be the truth," he said, "I promise."

I waited on the porch all morning. I waited, watching the sun on the ground and the flowers, the few cars that came down the street. The breeze came up midmorning and waved through the yard. The rosebushes shimmered in the heat and light. Dogs barked, quieted, barked again. Fidelio answered them from under the porch. Voices from across the street. I waited.

The telephone rang. I jumped and ran to the door to answer it. It was Ruth with a letter from Mother to read to me. I was polite and listened but couldn't wait for her to hang up. Before I went outside again, I went to the piano, lifted the lid and touched a few keys. The notes echoed in the silent living room. I noticed the piano was dusty and started to get a cloth to wipe it off.

The telephone again. I didn't move. Then I ran.

"Annie?" Father's voice. "Honey, it's all right. He's all right. The surgeon said the operation was a success as far as they can tell right now."

I couldn't speak.

"Annie? Are you there?"

"Yes, Father. Thank you. When can I see him?"

"Not for a while. He's still asleep and will be all day. Maybe in a few days. He's quite heavily bandaged right now to avoid infection. He'll look like the Invisible Man in that book for a while and he'll have some trouble eating. But he's fine."

I hung up the phone and then leaned against the wall. Slowly I slipped down until I was sitting on the floor. And while I sat there, for the first time I realized what it would have meant to me to lose Andrew.

18

I began spending more and more time at St. John's. I would rush through my morning errands: dishes, beds, a little straightening, cross the street, feed the chickens, see that Fidelio had water, pat him good-bye and then run to catch the trolley two blocks away. I didn't allow myself to think about what would happen when Mother came home, something I knew could happen any day. I knew that somehow Father and I would have to convince her that I should continue to go to St. John's. That I had lied to her and continued to lie with every letter I sent I didn't think about.

I also didn't admit to myself that I wasn't being truthful to Father. He still didn't know that I was disobeying Mother by going to the hospital. This summer had brought so many changes that I felt I could take care of only a few of them at a time. Father's return, Andrew, the other men at the hospital, my changed feelings for my friends, Grandfather's illness, Mother not understanding me—if I stopped to think about it all, I might lose control and spin away like someone thrown off the end of crack-the-whip.

I usually thought about all this in the early morning as I lay in bed and watched the sun cross my floor. I missed the sound of Mother's piano in the morning, the music that used to creep up the steps and under my door to tickle me awake. I missed Mother, our talks, her excited hugs, the fresh flowers she scattered around the house, her fiery bursts of anger and her instant forgiveness. But I also began to realize that life with Father had a different feeling from life alone with Mother. Days seemed more relaxed and freer with her gone. Maybe it was the evenings that lent the days their flavor. In the evenings, Father and I sat in the shelter of the porch and quietly talked about St. John's without worrying that Mother would overhear and disapprove.

A week after his surgery, Andrew's bandages were removed. Other than a new rawness about his mouth, he looked the same. He didn't talk about the operation and I didn't ask any questions. Soon he was able to eat and drink normally. I did ask Father if the operation had done what it was supposed to and he said it was too early to tell. He had said that this would go on for years and I wondered how it would feel to have to expect pain and discomfort for the rest of my life. I was impatient when I had a sore throat.

And then it was Timothy's turn. The day his bandages were coming off, I went out early to St. John's. Andrew and I sat on the patio while the doctors worked with Timothy. Andrew kept looking at the door and smoked so many cigarettes that the ashtray in front of him spilled out onto the table. I remembered what his mother had said about his smoking.

"What's the matter, Andrew? You didn't act like this before your bandages were taken off."

"Not the same thing at all. With me, it was just more of the same old thing. I didn't really expect any big change. But with Timothy . . . well, what if he can't see when they take off the last one? That's it, his last chance. And he knows it. That means that the damage hasn't healed and he'll be blind for life." He brushed at the table with his free hand.

This was the first time Andrew had talked about any-one's injuries but his own.

"You like him a lot, don't you?"

"Sure, he's a good kid. Awfully young, though."

He did seem younger than Andrew, even though Father had told me that they were probably about the same age, both about twenty-two. Timothy just seemed more like a little boy to me. Maybe it was the way he had to be helped to do so many things, like a child.

"Annie, when's your mom coming home?"

"What? Oh, I'm sorry . . . I was just thinking. I'm not sure. Could be any day now, I guess." I stacked the check-ers in piles of five. We hadn't been able to concentrate on a game. "Why?"

"Will you stop coming out to visit when she comes back? Maybe Timothy won't need to be read to anymore, and I know how your mother feels about . . ." He paused and stamped out his cigarette. "About me."

"I don't know. Do you think I should have done what she said? Obeyed her?"

"Of course not. I wouldn't've gotten to know you then." He grinned at me for a moment before he went on. "I think sometimes you have to do what you think is right, even if your folks don't agree. Sometimes you have to make up your own mind about things. Didn't you say that to me a while back?"

"Yes." I smiled down at the checkerboard. I wondered if he was thinking about his father. And I remembered what Uncle Paul had said that night at the opera, that Grandfather was always telling him what to do. The night I said he should do what he wanted to do. Maybe Uncle Paul and Andrew and I weren't so different after all.

"Annie." Andrew cleared his throat. "I think I found out something about your uncle."

I looked up at him. "What?" My mouth suddenly dried up.

"Remember you told me your uncle was killed at Belleau Wood on June sixth?"

I nodded.

"Well, something sounded wrong about it. But I wasn't sure so I didn't say anything. Then I got to talking to one guy who was in that battle, a Marine who was wounded near the end of June." He leaned forward and stretched his free hand out on the table between us. "Annie, I don't think your uncle was killed at Belleau Wood. On June sixth, the day he died, his company wasn't in battle. They were back of the lines, waiting for reinforcements. They didn't see any fighting until June fourteenth."

"So maybe he's alive?"

"Oh no, Annie. Don't think that. I'm sure he died. But maybe . . ."

"Tell me."

"Maybe he died some other way."

"What do you mean?"

"I don't know. I'm not sure. Maybe the date was just wrong. Someone sending the telegram made a mistake. But if your family wants the truth, there are probably men here who knew your uncle, who served with him. They probably don't realize you're related to him since you're a Metcalf and he was a MacLeod. So nobody ever said anything." He leaned forward. "But it just might be better to drop it, leave it as is and say they just made a mistake about the medal."

I pushed the checkers around the board and thought about what he had said. "No, I want to find out. Even if no one else does."

He looked at me for a moment and then said quietly, "OK, I'll ask around."

"Can I help? I'd like to talk to the men too."

"OK, if you're— Annie, you just might find out something you'd rather not know."

"What do you mean?"

"Men die in a lot of different ways during a war. I'm not saying that this happened to Paul, but if we start asking questions we might find out things that . . . Well, you set a lot of store by your uncle. Just be ready, OK?"

I nodded.

Andrew stood up. "They're taking a long time. I'm going in and see if Sister Anne knows anything."

"About what?"

He looked down at me. "Timothy, remember?"

"Oh, yes, I'll wait here." Before he left, he put his hand on my shoulder. "Don't worry ahead of time."

But I did. If Uncle Paul hadn't died the way the army said he did, what could have happened?

Andrew stood in the door, smiling. Before I could say anything, he grabbed my hand, pulled me out of my chair and hugged me.

"He can see!" He twirled me, almost lifting me off my feet. "He can see! Timothy's going to be all right!"

I couldn't breathe but I didn't care.

"Hey, listen, everybody!" he called out to the men under the trees. "Timothy's eyes are OK!" I leaned against him, dizzy for a moment. But I could hear them cheering.

19

Summer was disappearing faster than it ever had before. Mother's roses were at their peak, lush and velvety. I tried to prune and hoe them as I had seen her do every summer. I filled vases in the house with the heavy blooms and took others out to the hospital. The first day after Timothy's bandages were off, I took him a bunch of roses, and he held them out in front of him and then sniffed one gingerly.

"They look even better than they smell, Annie. I never thought I'd love to look at flowers so much."

I tried to ignore the calendar, tried not to notice how fast the time was running. Mother had been gone for a month now and I knew she would be home soon. And soon after that, school would start. Suddenly, school seemed like more of a loss of freedom than it ever had before. Even with all the books and maps and new things I wanted to learn. This summer I resented anything that stood between me and Andrew. I knew I would have to somehow fit my new life in with my old. I wasn't sure how to do that.

Timothy didn't seem as interested now in *Ivanhoe* as he had been before. Now many days when I got to St. John's in the afternoon he was playing the piano or playing ball with one of the other patients. Even when we sat down to start a new chapter, he stayed for only a little while and soon was up, pacing under the tree. He always apologized.

"I'm sorry, Annie. It's not you, or the story. I just can't

seem to sit still. I feel sometimes all I've done for a year is sit and do nothing. Maybe tomorrow." And he'd be gone, almost running out from under the shadows of our trees into the sunshine.

One afternoon, Andrew looked after him as he left swinging a baseball bat. When he turned and saw me watching him, he shrugged. "Well, I don't care much for *Ivanhoe* either right now. Any new atlases?"

"No, we've looked at all the ones the library has. Maybe when I go back to school . . ."

"That won't be long now, will it?"

"About a month." He was staring at his hands. "Don't worry. I'll still come out to see you. I'll bring my books and we can study together. I won't stop coming. I promise."

He tipped his head back against the bench.

"I used to hate going back to school. I loved summer, even though I had to work awful hard on the farm. But summer is warm and long and I had lots of fun."

"Didn't you like school? Ever?"

Andrew turned and looked at me, grinning. "Not much. Ever. I didn't like sitting still so long. I always wanted to be up and doing. Helping my dad. I was the only boy, so he needed me."

He'd never mentioned his father before.

"Where was your school?"

"In Stull. A little town about, oh, three miles from our place. Just a one-room place, one teacher, all of us jumbled in together. She didn't have much time for any of us. I learned to read and do my figures and that's about all." He looked at me again. "You're lucky, you know, Annie. You must have better teachers, if you like school so much."

"Yes, I guess I do."

"My sisters did better than I did. Sarah especially. She

141

wanted to be a teacher, but she ended up getting married. Now, well, I do like reading a bit now. I guess you got me started with your books. I've read a few copies of *National Geographic*. They're lying around inside there." He waved toward the hospital. "You're a good thing for me, Annie."

He spoke quickly, easily, and it took me a minute to realize what he had said. I looked up at him, to see if he was serious. He wasn't smiling, but looked back at me, his eyes sad.

I sat for a moment without speaking. I wanted to say something in return, to tell him that he was good for me too. Finally, I managed to say, "Thank you. I'm glad . . . I mean, I feel the same."

Then he said, "I've found a man who knew your uncle. His name is Henry Cook."

"Does he know about . . . ?"

"I didn't ask him. I didn't ask much of anything. I just overheard him talking about his company and it was the same as your uncle's, so I asked him if he knew Paul MacLeod. He did."

"Can we ask him?"

"Sure, if you want to. I don't know him at all, but we can ask."

As he was speaking, I realized that Andrew didn't seem to know many of the patients, that when I saw him he was either with Timothy or alone. And until last week, Timothy had been blind.

Andrew was watching me. "Annie, I have to warn you. Henry Cook was wounded, bad. His legs are . . . were . . . blown off."

I swallowed and nodded. "All right."

We found Henry Cook in the dining room playing solitaire on a board that lay across the arms of his wheelchair.

No one else was in the room. Our footsteps echoed around the empty high-ceilinged room, but Henry Cook didn't look up from the cards. As we got closer, I made myself look at him. A blanket covered his lap and the empty space where his legs and feet should be.

"Henry, this is Annie Metcalf, Dr. Metcalf's daughter."

He looked up slowly and then shaded his eyes with one hand. He nodded. "Hello. I've seen you around."

Andrew pulled up a chair for me and then sat to the side, out of the sunlight that splashed across the board on Henry's lap and the card game spread out on it.

"Henry, Paul MacLeod was Annie's uncle. That's why I asked if you knew him." Henry nodded. "Her family was told that he was killed at Belleau Wood. I wondered if you could tell Annie anything else, anything about her uncle."

Henry looked at me and then began to gather the cards into a stack. "I didn't know him, not really. I was in the third platoon. His was the second, I think."

"But you knew my uncle?"

"Yes. He was a good-enough lieutenant, seemed to worry over his men. One of my friends was in his platoon and he said Lieutenant MacLeod would do anything for his men—get them new boots, see they got hot food whenever he could." He looked at Andrew. "Not all officers were that way, right, Crayton?"

Andrew nodded. I could barely see his face where he sat.

For a minute the only sound was the sharp tap of the deck of cards on the board.

I decided Andrew was waiting for me to ask the question we were there to ask.

"Well, what I was wondering . . . You see, my uncle never got a Purple Heart. I guess you have one." He just

143

looked at me. "Anyway, Andrew says he should have one, if he was killed the way we were told he was. Like Lieutenant McFarland said."

"Lieutenant McFarland? What did he say?"

"He said my uncle was killed during the battle of Belleau Wood. And that he probably died trying to save one of his men."

"How do you know that isn't what happened?"

"Because he didn't get a medal. And the date is wrong."

"What date?"

"The telegram said he died on June sixth."

Henry put both elbows on the board and leaned forward. Then he turned to Andrew. "Crayton, maybe we should have a little talk."

"It's OK. I told her something might be wrong. But she really wants to find out. She's OK. You can tell her."

Henry looked down at the cards again, his mouth pulled to one side. He didn't speak for a long moment. I twisted my fingers in my lap. Then he said, "I don't really have anything to tell you. I mean, I don't know how your uncle died. But I do know that he wasn't with us at Belleau Wood. His platoon was behind us when we went in and there was a sergeant as platoon leader. Your uncle wasn't there."

"You're sure?"

"Yeah, I remember the men complaining, saying they wanted MacLeod back, they knew how he acted under fire and such. They'd been together since training here in the States." He shrugged. "Nothing they could do. And the sergeant was OK after all. But that telegram was wrong if it said he died in battle on June sixth."

I looked at Andrew. He put his hand to his mouth. Henry leaned both elbows on the arms of his chair and shifted, grunting as he moved. "We were back behind the lines on June sixth. We didn't see action until the fourteenth."

"Couldn't my uncle have been with another group?"

"Maybe." Henry frowned and shook his head. "Probably not though. They didn't move people around like that. Besides, no one, except the Marines, had been sent up yet. We was all sitting back waiting."

He glanced at me and then picked up the deck of cards and shuffled it. The fingers on his right hand seemed stiff and he dropped half the cards. He muttered something under his breath when I leaned forward to help him.

Henry spoke directly to me, leaning forward until his face was close to mine. "Don't worry about the medal, miss. It's not worth it. Just let it alone."

I stared at him without moving, but inside I was shaking my head. I couldn't go without knowing more. He had to know more, to tell me more about Uncle Paul. My uncle wouldn't leave his men without a good reason. There had to be a reason that I could find out.

Henry stared at the cards as he tapped them into a neat pile. "Crayton, if you really want to know what happened, talk to Lieutenant Owen. Eric Owen. A friend of MacLeod's. He was our platoon leader. He went back to HQ a few days before we were sent up the line." He gave the cards a final sharp tap. "When he got back, he told us Lieutenant MacLeod was dead." I held my breath.

"Wait a minute." Andrew bent over my shoulder toward Henry. "What do you mean?"

Henry looked up at him. "I mean he wasn't killed at the front."

I shook my head. "I don't understand . . ."

"Did Owen say how he died?"

Henry shrugged. "You better ask him."

"Where is he? Does he live in Kansas City?"

"He's here at St. John's. Got it the same time I did. Mortar attack. Hit smack in the middle of our platoon. Owen lost just one leg. Luckier than some of us. Five got killed." He paused. "You probably know him."

Andrew shook his head. "No, I don't."

Henry shifted in his chair. "Find Lieutenant Owen. He'll be able to tell you what you want to know."

"Thanks." Andrew turned to leave.

I stood up. My knees felt weak. I pushed the chair under the table and stood, my hands gripping the chairback.

Henry looked up at me. "Good luck. I hope you find out what you want to know."

I let go of the chair and held out my hand. "Thank you, Mr. Cook."

We shook hands; then I turned and walked from the room as quickly as I could.

"Wait a minute, Annie. Stop." I heard Andrew behind me.

I stood, my head down, wadding the sash of my middy blouse in my fist. Andrew put his hand on my shoulder. "Do you want to find Lieutenant Owen?"

I took a deep breath and looked up at Andrew. "I guess so."

"Are you all right?"

"Yes." I nodded. "Yes, I am."

"You want to find out more?"

I nodded. "Come on. Let's find Lieutenant Owen."

"OK. One of the sisters would know where he is."

But before we found a sister, my father found us.

"Annie! Great news!" He took both my hands and danced me in a half-circle. His face cracked with happiness. "Your mother just called. She's home!"

20

I stared at my father. He laughed at me. "Your mother is home. Don't look so mystified! Surely you remember your mother, Annie." He hugged me again. "Let's go. I can't wait to see her."

"Where is she?"

"Probably home by now. She called home from the station, and when no one answered she called Mark and Felicia to pick them up. She called here just before they left the station." As he talked, my father took off his white coat and emptied his pockets of instruments. Andrew and I stood and watched him.

My mother was home, but all I could think of was how I could convince my father that I had to stay here with Andrew and find Lieutenant Owen.

"Father, I . . ."

Suddenly, I felt Andrew's elbow in my side. "That's great, sir. I know how much you and Annie've missed her. I'll see you soon, Annie." He put his hand on my shoulder and turned to go.

"Wait. Andrew." I glanced at my father, but he was bent over the nurse's desk, his back to us. "What about Lieutenant Owen? Mother may not let me come back."

"What are you going to do? Hide out here? Go home and see your mom. You said you and your dad would change her mind. I'll find out about Lieutenant Owen, see where he is and if he'll talk to us. Don't worry, Annie. We'll keep after this."

"You find out. Then tell me."

"No. You need to hear it straight from him."

I looked down at my feet for a minute. "OK." I bit my lip. "Wait until I can get back."

"Gallant under fire, Annie." His voice, hoarse as always, was gentle. He must have known how frightened I was.

"Gallant under fire."

I spoke bravely, but as Father and I drove home on the motorcycle, I felt my stomach roll over and over. I would soon have to face Mother's anger. And it couldn't be put off. She would know immediately that I had been at St. John's with Father.

Father drove faster than usual and every time he glanced over his shoulder at me, he was grinning, his eyes laughing behind his goggles. I dreaded what he would think too when he found out that I had been lying all summer. I thought I had prepared myself for this moment, but now I was scared. I tried to think of Andrew's face and the picture of Uncle Paul, to remind me of why I had lied.

When we got home, Uncle Mark's Model T stood in front of my grandparents' house and luggage lay strewn on the grass. Father parked the motorcycle in our driveway and then grabbed my hand. "Come on, Annie." We ran across the street and up the steps to the door.

"Katherine!" He pulled open the door and then Mother was there and hugging us both at the same time, all of us laughing. Then Grandmother and Grandfather, stronger than when he left, surrounded us.

Everyone said I had grown, Father and I exclaimed over Grandfather's improvement, Grandmother made a weak attempt at unpacking. Finally, Aunt Felicia pushed us out the door, saying she'd take over and that Mother needed to get home to her own house. Mother said she just wanted to rest a bit since the train trip back had been exhausting.

I watched her as she laughed and pushed at her hair, noticing how brown she looked and the new turquoise ring she wore on her right hand. I wanted to be glad she was home, but I was afraid of her and of the questions she would ask.

She was too tired to do more than pat Fidelio, exclaim over her roses, glance at the stack of mail, and climb the steps to her room. Father went up with her and then came down, saying she had fallen asleep. He asked me to stay with her while he went back to St. John's.

"I'll try to be back early, Annie. You help your mother when she wakes up."

"Father . . ."

He looked at me, his foot on the starter pedal of the motorcycle. "What is it, Annie?"

"Nothing." I leaned over and kissed him on the cheek. "If you see Andrew, tell him not to worry."

He frowned at me. "Worry? About what?"

"Nothing." I smiled and waved and he kicked the motorcycle pedal down and wheeled out of the driveway.

Mother slept for two hours. I sat on the porch, a book in my hand, trying to read. Every time I lifted the book and stared at the page, I saw Andrew, or Henry Cook. Or heard my mother saying I wasn't to go back to St. John's. I remembered how she had turned her back on Andrew and every word of the terrible argument we had had when we got home. The only good part of that day, the only part I could remember without my stomach spinning, was my talk with Ruth that evening on my grandparents' porch. I wished Ruth were here to help me now.

I read one paragraph three times before I finally shut the book and set it beside me on the swing. I wondered what Andrew was doing.

The screen door swung open. Mother stood in the doorstep, yawning, her hair loose down her back.

"Hello, darling." She bent over and kissed me, her familiar smell of perfume and powder surrounding me. She stood and wound her hair around her head and pinned it. "Ohhh." She fanned herself with her hand. "It is *so* much hotter here. The mountains are delightfully cool."

Muffin jumped onto the porch railing in front of her. "Oh, hello, kitty." She lifted the cat to her face and nuzzled him against her cheek. "I missed you." I could hear the cat purring from where I sat.

"You want to come help me unpack? And you can tell me what you've done to keep busy while I've been gone."

I followed her into the hall where Father had dropped her luggage.

"Why did you come home so suddenly?" I asked.

She knelt by the suitcase and unsnapped the locks. "You know your grandfather. He just woke up yesterday and announced that he wanted to come home." She shook out her dresses and handed them to me. "Would you hang these on the line to air out? Frankly, I was ready to come home. I missed you and your father. And mountains are tiresome after a while." I could hear her voice as I walked through the house and to the backyard. Maybe I could keep her talking about Colorado until Father came home.

"Did you take any hikes?"

"A few. Your grandfather was in no shape . . . Oh, look, Annie, what I found for your father." She pulled out a long package and handed it to me. It was heavy. As I unrolled it, a rug, woven in bright colors, fell into my

150

lap. "It's an Indian rug. They bring them up from New Mexico and Arizona. Isn't it beautiful?"

"I've never seen anything like it." I ran my hand over the rough surface and combed my fingers through the fringe.

"I thought we could hang it on the wall of his office. Or here at home. And I have something for you." She reached into the side pocket of her suitcase and brought out a small white box. "Here."

I opened the lid, and lying on the cotton was a silver bracelet with three small turquoise stones. I slipped it over my wrist.

"Do you like it?"

I looked up at my mother where she sat, her clothes strewn around her on the wood floor. She smiled at me, waiting for me to tell her how much I loved the bracelet. It was too much. My hand closed around the silver band and tears began to run down my face. Instantly, she had her arms around me. "Annie, dear, what is the matter?"

"Oh, Mother. I can't tell you."

"What, Annie? Tell me." She reached behind her. "Here." She handed me a handkerchief.

I wiped at my eyes. "I've been lying to you all summer. I've been doing what you told me not to do. But I've got to keep going out there. I just have to. No matter what you say."

Mother sat back on her heels. "Annie, tell me what you're talking about. Now."

I took a breath. "I've been going out to St. John's almost every day since you've been gone, to visit Andrew. And I've been reading to Timothy, taking up where Grandfather left off. I've gone almost every day since you left." I stopped talking and looked down at the bracelet that

151

circled my wrist and my hands that were clamped into fists in my lap. Then I lifted my head to look at Mother.

She stood up, sweeping the rest of her clothes into her arms. She turned and walked to the basement door and switched on the light. "Annie, would you empty the food basket? It's there by the door." And she went downstairs.

I stood alone in the hall. She hadn't said anything. But I knew she would. As I picked up the basket, I noticed my hands were shaking. I clasped them together to make them stop, then went to the kitchen, opened the basket and put away the fruit. While I worked, I listened for sounds from downstairs. When I heard Mother's footsteps on the stairs, I went back into the living room to wait for her.

She stooped to gather the rest of her things and then closed the lid of the suitcase. "You can take it downstairs now." I started for the door. "But before you go . . ." I stopped, my back to her.

"You never mentioned this in your letters."

I shook my head.

"Annie, look at me."

I turned and looked at her.

"In other words . . ."

"I lied."

"You lied to me all summer. And you deliberately disobeyed me."

I nodded.

"Why?"

"Because you were wrong."

The words echoed between us.

She stared at me.

"And because Andrew needed me, needs me. And Timothy. And because they aren't terrible or awful the way

152

you and everyone else seems to think. They fought, just like Uncle Paul! They were brave like he was. They can't help what happened to them! Andrew can't help it that he was hurt. Why can't you see that? His own father won't come to see him! But I will. He's my friend and I'm going back out there again."

Mother straightened her shoulders and lifted her chin a little. We stood facing each other.

"I am, Mother."

"Annie." She seemed about to say something and then stopped. "We'll talk about this more when your father comes home. I don't want to hear any more now."

Father came home early. Mother had gone out to prune her roses and also, I think, to avoid me. I stayed up in my room until I heard the roar of the motorcycle. Then I came slowly down the stairs. I knew Mother would talk to Father immediately. When she was angry, she didn't wait. She couldn't cover her feelings and pretend everything was all right.

When I came out on the porch, she was sitting in the wicker rocker, rocking hard. Father stood by the railing, hands in his pockets.

"Hello, Annie."

"Annie, go get your father a glass of iced tea, please. After that we'll talk."

They hadn't moved when I returned; they didn't speak. I handed Father the glass and sat in the swing. Muffin jumped into my lap.

"I guess we have a problem, Annie." Father sat down on the railing, one hand tapping his knee. "Your mother tells me she isn't happy about the way you've spent the summer."

"No, sir."

"Lawrence, you make it sound so silly. Here I've been in Colorado, all this time thinking Annie is safe, tucked away in the library with her books, or with her friends. Now I find out she's been spending her days with a group of . . . of . . ." She raised her hands and let them drop in her lap.

"Of what, Katherine?"

"I don't know."

"Katherine, Andrew is a young soldier who was badly gassed in the Argonne. His face was burned, and his hands and torso. He's had plastic surgery on his face and they're working on his hands now in therapy."

Mother's hands were clenched in front of her, knuckles white. "What does he look like?" she asked quietly. I looked at her. She knew what Andrew looked like. She had seen him that day she came to the hospital.

"Like most burn patients, he has a lot of scar tissue. His eyes are all right, but his nose is partially gone and his mouth only partially reconstructed. He had some surgery a few weeks ago. The surgeon doesn't know yet if he'll need more."

Mother nodded. She didn't look at me. "Go on."

"His face looks pretty angry now, red and sore. In time, the high color will fade. But he will never have a normal face. The scarring is very deep and the features will never be normal."

"And *this* is the man Annie is going to see?"

"He's not just any man, Mother. He's my friend." My voice shook.

"I don't—"

"Katherine, let me finish. You said you had trusted my judgment. Hear me out, please. I believe that Annie has been very important to Andrew's recovery. Before she began to visit him, he was very withdrawn, very bitter. Now he's made friends with Timothy Lewis, who, by the way, has recovered his sight."

Despite my churning stomach, despite my hands that shook as I smoothed them on my skirt, I wanted to run out on the street and sing at the top of my voice. Father said I was important for Andrew, that I had helped him, that I was good for him—Andrew's words.

"And Andrew seems to be making more of an effort to socialize with the other men. His mother has told me that she can see the difference."

"I still don't see—"

"I know you don't see. You've never come to visit, so you don't know what the men are doing or how they look or, most importantly, what kind of people they are." I looked up at Father. He only used that clipped tone of voice when he was really angry.

"I know, Larry. But you know how I feel, how I am about things like that." Mother turned away from us and looked out into the cooling yard. "I can't face it," she whispered. "You can't ask that of me." She stood up and walked to the edge of the porch.

"I'm not asking you to face it. I'm asking you to try to understand why it is important that you let Annie face it."

"Mother, when I first saw Andrew, I was afraid too. I actually ran away." I looked at Father, who was staring into his glass. "But once I got to know him . . . it's like I've forgotten there's anything wrong. It's just, it's Andrew's face, that's all."

Father looked at me, half smiling. Mother stood without moving, her back to us. I stepped toward her. "Mother,

I didn't like disobeying you, really. But . . . I had to."

"I don't know. I don't know." Mother stood, her hands pressed to her cheeks. "It's not that I blame Andrew, as you seem to think I do. That's not it. I do feel terribly sorry for him . . . and all the others." She turned around suddenly. "I just want to *forget* all of this. It must end sometime. All the pain and hurt. Isn't it enough that we lost Paul?" She turned around suddenly. "Must we always remember?"

Father just looked at her.

"Andrew can't forget." I spoke so quietly I almost couldn't hear the words myself. I wondered if I'd really said the words or just thought them. But I had said them because Mother turned and looked at me. She looked like she was about to speak, but she only walked slowly to the door, opened it, shut it again. She stood a moment, her back to us, before she turned and looked first at Father and then at me.

"Obviously, I have nothing to say about this." And she went inside and shut the door behind her.

21

That evening, after a dinner where we all talked carefully about Mother's trip and Grandfather's health, we crossed the street to visit my grandparents. But even seeing Grandfather looking so healthy and being able to tell him that Timothy could see again didn't help me forget the anger that had spilled over and spoiled the homecoming. Lying in my bed that night, I thought how much I had missed them. But now, just as when Father returned home last spring, the reunion wasn't as joyful as it should have been. I remembered how I felt the day Father came home, how frightened I had been of what I had seen at the train station, how afraid I had been of those men whose faces looked so horrible. And now again those wounded men had come between me and my family. But this time I wasn't the one who was afraid. It was my mother.

I pulled the curtains back from the window to get all the breeze I could and stared out the window onto the yard. What if Uncle Paul were out there? Would Mother go to see him? Even if he looked like Andrew?

I leaned over to my dresser and took down the picture. I couldn't see it very well in the darkness, only a dim outline. But I knew what it looked like: eyes, smile, dark hair, the happiness that surrounded him. I covered the picture with my hand. "Oh, Uncle Paul, why can't you still be alive?"

And I wondered if Andrew's mother had a picture on her mantel in Stull, a picture of Andrew, helping her remember him before he went away.

I stayed by the window a long time that night, unable to sleep.

The next morning when I woke up, it took me a moment to remember why the picture lay on the windowsill. As I reached over to get it, I heard the piano. I lay back and listened to the music as it curled up from the floor below. Quiet music, gentle. I tried to guess how Mother felt from the way she played. Hard to tell. I dressed and ran downstairs to find Father. I wanted to tell him what we'd learned from Henry Cook, but when I saw him I decided not to. He didn't seem in a mood to talk so I just asked, "Father, will you take a message to Andrew?"

He just looked at me.

"Tell him that I'll try to get out as soon as I can."

Father squeezed his eyes shut and rubbed his forehead with his fingertips. Then he sighed. "OK, I'll tell him. But Annie, for me, for your mother, will you stay home today? Maybe that will help—"

"I'd already decided to. I wasn't going out to the hospital at all."

He stood up and set his coffee cup on the shelf behind him. "Thanks, Annie. We'll see this one out."

I watched through the window while Father wheeled out the motorcycle and started the motor. While he was adjusting his goggles, Mother came out of the house and they talked for a few minutes. I sighed. Maybe a good sign.

I heard her footsteps on the porch. "Good morning, Annie."

I turned. "Hi, Mother."

And the morning began. Mother stood in the living room and exclaimed over all the cleaning there was to be done in the house. We were polite with each other, but didn't speak much. Midmorning, Ruth called and Mother asked her to come over after lunch.

After she hung up, Mother stood with her hand on the phone and turned to me. "When Ruth comes, you can go out to St. John's."

I stopped moving, the dustcloth in my hand halfway to the dinner table. "What?"

She smoothed her apron and walked into the living room. "You heard what I said."

I followed her, but stopped in the doorway, still holding the dustcloth. "I'm not going out there today. I told Father—"

"Don't you usually go every day?" Her back was to me as she arranged the sofa cushions.

I nodded and cleared my throat so I could speak. "Yes, most every day."

"Well, don't let my coming home ruin your plans." She straightened, her back still to me. "No, that's not what I meant to say." She turned suddenly, one hand at her waist, the other at her forehead. "Annie, I'm still very angry over what you did." She sat down suddenly on the sofa as if her knees had buckled. "But . . ." She sighed and put her hand to her forehead again. "I didn't get much sleep last night for thinking about this."

I thought of us both, awake and angry.

"I know you think I'm being a coward, and not very understanding. I'm not the strong person your father is. But try to understand that I am thinking of you. Being with such badly wounded men, no matter how nice they are, can't help but be disturbing."

I opened my mouth to disagree, but she held up her hand. "I don't want to argue about it. I just know how

159

upsetting"—and she paused and took a deep breath before she went on—"this can be. But your father said this was important and that I shouldn't stand in your way. So even though I don't want you to go, I won't stop you." She spoke quickly, as if to get the words out before she changed her mind.

"Thank you, Mother." I didn't say anymore and went back to dusting. But inside, I rejoiced. I rushed through the rest of my chores and ran to the trolley stop.

On the trolley, as I sat with hands clenched in my lap, I remembered. This was the first time I had gone to St. John's without my bookbag. I leaned back and took a deep breath. Why was I so nervous? Why did I feel that my hands and feet might fail me if I didn't concentrate very hard on keeping steady?

Because Andrew would have found Lieutenant Owen, if he was still at St. John's. Because today I was going to find out how my uncle died. And suddenly I wished I had never started this, had never seen Andrew's Purple Heart and begun to ask questions.

The hospital looked as it always did, trees, shadows, curving pathway. Only a few men sat outside, since it was lunchtime. Then I saw him, sitting on the bench where we had first met, sitting as he did so often, alone, hands on his knees.

"Hello, Andrew."

"Annie, what are you doing here? I thought . . ."

"She let me come. She's still angry, but . . ." I shrugged. "I don't understand my mother very often."

"I know how you feel." He patted the bench beside him. "Sit down."

"Did you find him?"

He sighed and looked out over the grass. Then he nodded. "Yes."

160

"Did you ask him?"

He nodded again.

"Well?"

"Annie, let's find your father and then go talk to Owen. Don't worry, it's not horrible or . . . anything. But it might upset you and I want—"

"No, I want to hear it first and then we'll tell Father. Please. No one else thought this was important except you. So let's finish it together."

He slowly got to his feet. "OK. We'll do it your way. Come on. He's inside, in the wards."

"Can I go in there?"

"Should be OK. Everyone else is at lunch."

"Why isn't he?"

"He's a lot worse hurt than Cook said. A shell punctured his lungs. You'll see."

I did when I met Lieutenant Owen. I could hear his breathing as soon as we entered the long bright room, could hear the rasp in his throat before we were halfway to his bed in the far corner. When we got near him, I saw that he half lay, half sat against pillows, his arms out over the covers and the sheet draped carefully over his leg.

Andrew bent over him and touched his hand. "Lieutenant Owen. It's Andrew Crayton. I've brought Annie."

The man on the bed nodded and reached out to me. Going past Andrew to the bed, I took his hand. It was thin and made me think of my grandfather.

"Glad to meet you, Annie. To know some of Paul's family. I had no idea . . ." Suddenly he began to cough, his body arching forward. He let go of my hand and covered his mouth with a cloth, pressing it hard against his lips. I glanced over my shoulder at Andrew.

"Can I get him some water?"

Andrew shook his head. "No, just wait."

After a moment, Lieutenant Owen gave one final cough and fell back on his pillows. "All over. I'm sorry." He thumped a hand on his chest and let out a gust of air. "Old lungs don't operate so well. Crayton, find a chair for Annie. There's one over there."

Andrew brought two chairs and sat behind me. I pulled my chair close to the bed. The man's weak voice was hard to hear even in the silent room.

"Lieutenant Owen—"

"Please call me Eric. Makes me feel a perfect ancient to have a pretty girl call me by my last name."

"Eric—"

"I had no idea your dad was related to Paul. Quite a fellow, Paul. Brave, got the Bronze Star, you know. That was for action we saw that spring." He paused and turned his head to look out the window. In the silence, I heard voices as men came out of the dining room onto the terrace.

Eric's hands moved a little, fingers curling on the sheet. He looked back at me. "A good officer. Knew how to get the boys to move, never had problems with the men. Good officer." He turned again to the window.

"Eric—"

"And a good friend. We had fun. He loved music, knew all the new tunes . . ." I could barely hear him and I leaned forward to be closer as he looked at the sunlight on the trees outside his window. He coughed twice, but more quietly than before. The room was still around us.

Suddenly I was afraid he would fall asleep, he had grown so quiet.

"Eric, how did my uncle die? Do you know?"

He didn't move for a minute, and I moved my hand forward to touch his arm. Then he looked back at me. "I was with him. They let me stay with him, even though he didn't know me at the end. He was burning up, delirious."

I looked back at Andrew.

Andrew shook his head and put a finger to his lips.

"They said they couldn't do anything for him. Just then, the hospital began to get the wounded Marines from the front. So they put him in a corner. Told me they couldn't do anything. No medicine for it."

"Medicine for what? What did he die of? Was he wounded?"

Eric moved his head back and forth on the pillow. "No, no, he wasn't wounded. He was sick. Measles."

"Measles?" Again I looked at Andrew. "But what did he die of?"

Eric frowned at me. "Die of? The fever caused by the measles." He coughed once, twice. "I'm sorry."

I almost laughed. I pulled back from the bed and shook my head. "That can't be true. I don't believe you. Uncle Paul couldn't have—"

"Annie . . ." I felt Andrew's hand on my shoulder.

"Sorry, I'm sorry." Eric kept repeating the word, over and over. He reached out and took my hand. I stood up, the chair tipping over behind me. Still he held on to my hand. "It doesn't matter. Don't forget, your uncle was—"

"No!" I stepped back from the bed, pulling my hand out of Eric's weak grip. I stared down at him. I couldn't seem to catch my breath. I knew I should thank him, should be sorry because it seemed to upset him to talk about my uncle, should apologize for being rude. But all I could say was "No, no, no." And before Andrew could stop me, I turned and ran down the aisle between the empty beds and the tall windows, ran out the front door of the hospital into the hot sun.

22

I crouched on the bench, shivering, arms clenched tightly around me, eyes shut against the glare. Shivering in the hot August sun. My uncle couldn't have died that way, of a sickness, a silly disease that babies got, that I'd had when I was four. Anyway, Lieutenant Owen was sick, he dreamed things. This was a story he'd imagined. He'd forgotten how Uncle Paul died. If he really knew. If anyone really knew.

I felt someone's arms around me. Andrew. The bandages on his left hand scratched my arm as he pulled me closer to him. He didn't speak, just kept his arm around me until I stopped shaking.

"Annie, does it matter so much?"

"What he said can't be true."

"Why not?"

"Because they told us he died helping his men. How could he get measles? He was a grown-up. He wouldn't have gone off just because he got a few measles. Not when his men needed him."

"Annie, he couldn't help getting sick. A lot of men did over there. And even things like measles were real serious when they couldn't get good care. And so men died of all kinds of things. It just happened."

I didn't want to cry so I clenched my eyes, my lips, my hands.

He asked me again, "Does it matter so much how he died?"

"Yes."

"Why?"

"Because . . . then he isn't . . ."

"A hero?"

"Yes."

"And if he isn't?"

"It doesn't make any sense."

"What doesn't?"

"That he died," I whispered.

"Oh, Annie." Quietly. And then neither of us spoke, but sat together. And I was glad he was there. Then he started to speak, so softly that at first his words were only part of the air. But after a while I began to listen. "Dying is always hard, especially if it's the death of someone you love. Now you have to see Paul's death in a different way. But dying from measles is no worse than dying in combat. And no better. That he had to die at all is . . . what doesn't make sense."

I looked down at his hand on my arm, his hand that was still wrapped in bandages. I realized suddenly that the bandages didn't make any sense either, that Andrew hadn't been heroic when he lost his gas mask and was burned in that forest. Finally I did begin to cry.

"I'm sorry." I pulled back from him and repeated, "I'm sorry."

"What do you mean?"

I didn't know what to tell him. I knew no words to tell him.

Father and I left the hospital early that day. As we walked together to the motorcycle, I told him what we'd learned. He didn't say anything, but he put his arm around me. Suddenly I felt exhausted and could barely climb on the back of the motorcycle. I leaned my cheek against his broad warm back as the afternoon air whipped around us. My head ached and my eyes burned. I felt I could sleep for days.

When we pulled into the driveway, we heard the piano. Ruth must have left and Mother was home alone. I glanced at Father as he bent to lock up the motorcycle. We hadn't had the time to talk much about this. Maybe I could get upstairs to my room before she saw me.

But the music stopped as I opened the kitchen door and stepped into the cool house. I knew she would see me but hoped it was dark enough so she wouldn't notice my face. Through the hall, into the living room.

She sat at the piano, turning pages. She looked up. "Annie. I didn't hear . . . Annie!"

She half rose from the piano, but all I could see was her silhouette against the window. I heard her call my name again before I slammed the door to my room.

I lay on my bed for hours, it seemed. How long could it take for Father to tell her? Then I remembered that she knew nothing about any of this—the Purple Heart, the wrong date, Henry Cook, Lieutenant Owen. None of the things that had seemed important to me all summer. So he would need a long time. The shadow of the house was deep into the backyard before I heard her steps on the stairs. And then a knock on my door. I had to say "come in" twice before the door opened.

Mother looked like I felt. She had been crying too. As I lay on the bed, we looked at one another; then she shut the door behind her and walked slowly to my rocking chair and sat down. She pulled a handkerchief between her hands.

When she spoke, her voice wasn't steady. "Your father

told me about . . . what you found out today." She didn't look at me.

I didn't say anything.

"I had no idea that was how Paul died," she whispered. "I wish now I didn't know. You see now why I didn't want you to go out there. Things get stirred up that are better left alone. It just goes on . . . and on." She waved her hand and then held the handkerchief to her eyes. After a minute, she half gasped, half sobbed, "It just isn't fair."

I sat up straight and wiped my face against my sleeve. "Mother, how would you feel if Uncle Paul had been gassed like Andrew and was out at St. John's right now?" I stood up. "Would you feel better then?"

"Annie, I . . ." Mother put her hand to her throat.

"You know what? All this time I'd been worrying about whether Uncle Paul died like a hero. It really doesn't matter. That's what Andrew said. The only thing that matters is that he's dead. One way or the other . . . all the same. None of it makes any sense to me."

Mother pressed the handkerchief to her mouth.

"Do you know why Andrew was burned? He lost his gas mask in a battle. When the gas came, he looked for the mask and it was gone. And so he was burned so badly he wanted to die. Was that fair? He told me he would have shot himself if they hadn't taken away his gun. But all I could ever think about was my dead uncle, how brave he was. How do you think that made Andrew feel? He probably wishes he had died over there instead of coming home looking like he does, instead of coming home when the heroes all died. And then Uncle Paul didn't die the way we thought, not helping someone. Not brave and splendid. He got sick and died because nobody could take care of him. None of it is any fair at all."

I stood by my bed, holding on to the bedpost, facing her across the dim blueness of my room.

"Mother, all we have of Uncle Paul are memories. But Andrew's alive. He's *here*. And all the other men out at St. John's. And it doesn't seem right to me that you and everybody else just want to forget them. That's what I don't understand. *That's* what isn't fair."

Mother let out a sobbing breath and covered her face with both hands. I knelt beside her and put my arms around her. And in the darkening room we cried together, for Paul and what we had lost in him. And maybe too for Andrew and all the others.

23

That night I went to sleep immediately. I had thought I wouldn't, that I would lie awake as I had the night before. But after Mother left me, I lay down on the bed and fell asleep at once. I awoke the next morning, still in my clothes from the day before.

I lay in bed, knowing that something was changed from other mornings, but for a moment I couldn't remember what had happened. Then yesterday flooded over me and I buried my face in the pillow. Uncle Paul. No longer bravely sacrificing himself. Now dying in a corner, all alone, hot with fever, unable to recognize his friend.

I turned my head on the pillow and looked at his picture. Same smile, same tilt of the head. That Uncle Paul, the one I had come to know the spring before he went to France, hadn't changed. Uncle Paul's death made no sense, but his life still meant the same to me.

I turned over on my back and listened. No sound from below, no piano, no talking. I wondered how Mother was, if she had slept at all.

When I found her, she was bending over the roses, pruning the long canes and the dead blossoms I had missed. She greeted me quietly, asked me what I'd like for breakfast. She looked tired.

While I ate, we talked about what I needed for school and planned a trip to town to shop. She mentioned having Emily and Darby over for an afternoon and then she said, "If you have time. I know you usually go to the hospital in the afternoon."

I only nodded, my eyes on my plate.

"Well," she said, "we'll see if we can work it out."

She took a sip of coffee and traced the pattern of the tablecloth with her finger. "Your father and I talked last night. We think it's better if we don't say anything about . . . about Paul to your grandparents. Maybe in time, Dad will be strong enough. But I don't think your grandmother need ever know." She looked up at me. "All right?"

"I understand. I won't say anything."

Mother stood up. "She'll be happier, I know." And she began to clear the table. "I'll tell Mark and John when they come out on Sunday."

I sat at the table watching her. If I hadn't asked questions, if I had never seen that beautiful dark Purple Heart, none of us would be in such pain. I didn't feel any regret that I had discovered the truth, but I wished I could help her as Andrew had helped me.

I stood up. "Mother . . . " I stepped toward her.

She turned from the sink.

I set my cup down. "I'll finish the dishes."

A few days later, I asked Andrew if we could visit Eric Owen again and ask him more about Uncle Paul.

"That's not a good idea, Annie," Andrew said. "He's not very well right now."

"How sick is he?"

"You better ask your dad. He's the doctor."

When I asked Father, he didn't answer for a minute. Then he said, "He probably won't live very long, Annie. Andrew's right. You shouldn't see him again."

I thought of him though, and remembered him lying on his white bed, coughing. I wished I had asked him more, had talked to him more while I had the chance. No one told me when he died.

Timothy was leaving, going to live with his sister in St. Louis. He had finished his treatment and the doctors were sure that his recovery would last, that his eyes were fully healed. He met me on the path one afternoon when I was looking for Andrew and he told me the news.

"Ask your grandfather to come out. I haven't seen him since he got home, and I want to before I go."

"OK, I will. We never did finish *Ivanhoe*, did we?" He shrugged and grinned. "Timothy, have you seen Andrew today?"

"He's probably on the wards. He's been helping with some of the bed patients. Ask one of the sisters."

I went in the front door into the quiet shadowy hall leading down to the dining room. Voices echoed, footsteps, doors closing—all the sounds that were so familiar to me by now. And the smell—the mixture of soap and alcohol that always clung to my father's clothes when he came home. All this had become so familiar to me over the summer, as St. John's had become a part of my life.

A nun crossed the hall. "Excuse me, Sister Elizabeth."

She paused and smiled. "Hello, Annie."

"Have you seen Andrew Crayton?"

"Oh, yes, he's busy on the wards. He's started working with the amputees, doing some therapy, you know. I'm afraid he won't be able to visit today, dear."

"Oh." I felt immensely foolish and embarrassed. "That's all right. I just wondered . . ."

"Shall I tell him you're here?"

"No, that's all right. I have to get home anyway."

But I didn't. I sat outside, on our bench, all afternoon. I had books with me and I read. But I kept watching the door to the hospital, hoping that Andrew would come, that the sister would tell him after all, or that he would look out a window and see me, or that he would just come out in hopes that I was there. I felt a little hurt that he was busy, that he found things to fill his afternoons without me. But the shadows grew and the afternoon cooled around me and then Father came to take me home.

"All alone, Annie? Where's Andrew?"

I waved vaguely toward the hospital. "Inside. He's got some kind of a job, or something."

Father picked up my bookbag and slung it over his arm as we walked toward the motorcycle. "Oh, yes, I forgot, he's learning how to do dressings and bandaging. Good training."

"For what?"

"Oh, for later on." He bent to unlock the motorcycle. "Sorry you came out for nothing."

Later that evening while I was helping Mother with the dishes, the telephone rang. Father called to me, "Annie, for you."

Mother and I looked at each other, she with her eyebrows raised, me with my mouth open. I never got phone calls.

"Annie, it's Andrew." His voice sounded deeper over the wire. I felt I was talking to a stranger. "Are you there?"

"Yes. Hi."

"I'm sorry I missed you today. Sister Elizabeth told me you were waiting for me. I should have told you I'd be busy a lot now in the afternoons."

"That's OK. Don't worry." I wanted to ask if he meant every afternoon.

He went on. "You'll be busy with school soon, anyway."

"Yes."

"Listen, Annie, Timothy is leaving day after tomorrow. Can you come out tomorrow? We're planning to celebrate."

"Won't you be busy?"

"No, no, they'll let me sneak away for this." He sounded so happy, chuckling as he spoke. And I felt I could cry. "Anyway, can you come?"

"Timothy already asked me to bring Grandfather out."

"Great idea. It'll be swell to see him again."

"What time?"

"Oh, in the afternoon. We're getting up a baseball game. We've been practicing for a couple of weeks. Decided it's time for a real game. See if Timothy's as good as he's been bragging. It should be fun." The words tumbled out over the phone.

"Annie?"

"What?"

"I am sorry I couldn't see you today. Do you understand?"

"I guess so. I'll see you tomorrow."

I hung up the phone carefully and then leaned my head against the wall for a minute. Everything was changing. Even the air that blew in the front door was cool with autumn. I didn't want things to change. I wanted this summer to go on forever, with things just like they were.

Then Mother called to me from the living room, asking who had been on the phone. I told them about Timothy leaving and the plans for the next day. "We'll take the trolley out."

"I'll drive you both out," Mother said. "I have to go to town anyway." We both looked at her but she was absorbed in stirring her coffee. Father looked up at me and winked.

Mother dropped us off at the gate. Grandfather asked her to come in, saying that Timothy would love to see her again. But she just shook her head.

"No, but tell him good-bye for me. And good luck."

"That I will, Katherine." Grandfather opened the car door. "Coming, Annie?"

"Thanks for the ride, Mother," I said as I climbed out. Then I leaned through the window and kissed her cheek.

"You're welcome." She retied her veil under her chin. "Say hello to Andrew as well."

She drove off quickly.

I stood in the street, looking after her in wonder. I knew I had heard her correctly. Grandfather called to me and we walked slowly up the path to the hospital. On the grass where I had first met Andrew, the baseball game had already started. Patients and nuns stood on the slope to watch. As Grandfather and I walked out from under the trees, the man up at bat swung and missed and the men in the outfield cheered.

"Grandfather, that's Timothy pitching!"

"You're right. He's a crackerjack man with a slow pitch."

Grandfather and I stood and watched him strike out the next man. Then one of the patients noticed us and made room for us on the bench. I looked for Andrew but couldn't find him until he took off his hat to wipe his face on his sleeve. He was standing by third base, watching the pitcher. I waved my hat, but he didn't notice, because just then a ball looped through the air and a man in the outfield caught it. The other team was out and Timothy and Andrew trotted toward home plate. When Timothy saw us, he handed his glove to another player and ran over to us.

"Welcome home, sir. Good to see you." He shook Grandfather's hand. "Hi, Annie. Good game, right? We're ahead, three to two." The sun danced in his face and in his eyes.

"Can Andrew play?" We all looked at him as he talked to the man getting ready to bat.

"Nope, he's our manager. Does a good job. Oops, gotta go. I'm up. I'll see you in a minute as soon as I strike out."

But he didn't strike out. He made it to second base before a man with an eye patch caught the ball and tagged him.

Around us the men cheered and whistled, calling jokes to each other. My father and another doctor came out to watch, and before long they were playing.

Grandfather leaned back on the bench and crossed his arms. "Oh, I wish I were younger. I'd show 'em how to play ball."

But Timothy and Andrew didn't need any help to beat the other team. They won—nine to six. All the men shook hands and praised each other's playing.

One of the nuns who had come out to watch announced that ice cream was ready on the porch. More laughing and cheering. As we walked back toward the hospital, the men quieted down. With dishes in hand, they scattered out under the trees where I'd watched them so often before. But I still heard drifts of talk and catches of laughter.

The nuns had made peach ice cream, and the chunks of fruit tasted a bit sour as I bit into them. Andrew, Timothy and I sat on the wall surrounding the porch, while Grandfather, Father and several other doctors sat at the tables. The nuns hovered, never sitting, but constantly checking on everyone's happiness.

"How do you like that motorcycle of yours, Larry?" asked one of the doctors. "Work all right?"

"Sure does. I enjoy it a lot. And I've had no trouble. Works like a charm."

"I worry about the safety," said another doctor. "Doesn't seem very secure."

"Depends on the driver." Everyone turned to look at

175

Andrew. His face turned a little redder than usual. But he went on. "A good driver is OK. But if you're careless you'll have problems."

"Have you ridden?" Father asked.

"Some. One of my friends in school bought a motorcycle. And then in the army. I was a messenger for a while here in the States while we were in training."

"Would you like to try mine?"

Andrew paused only a moment before he nodded, a huge grin on his face.

So we all followed Father around to the back of the hospital where he parked his motorcycle. He bent and unlocked it and adjusted the seat. Andrew carefully climbed onto the bike and eased down onto the seat. He put his hand out to the handlebars and again tried to grip with his bandaged hand. He looked up at Father.

"Wait a minute, Andrew. Here." Father wrapped a rag around the end of the handlebar, making it fatter so that Andrew's hand fit snugly about it. After showing him where the gears and brakes were, Father stepped back.

"Just take a short ride, Andrew. Around the lot here. We don't want to damage that hand."

When Andrew kicked the motorcycle on, we all stepped back. He looked down at the gears and then up at us. He was smiling, the broadest smile I'd ever seen on his face. He lifted his hand, almost in a salute, and drove off in a wide arc, around the cars parked in rows. As I watched, I raced with him in my mind, feeling the wind on his face and in his hair, feeling the ground below and the warm air around and the sun above.

"Did you ever think we'd see such a sight as that, Annie?" Father said.

I shook my head.

Andrew rode for a while, then Timothy took a turn, then several other patients, then Andrew again. After he parked the motorcycle for the last time, I helped him with the lock. His eyes were still shining, but in the gathering shadows his face looked drawn, the droop of his eyes and mouth stronger. He looked tired.

"Are you OK?" I whispered to him.

"Yes, don't say anything. I don't want your dad to worry. I'm exhausted, but it was sure worth it." He patted the motorcycle, and together we walked back and found Timothy and Grandfather at the table.

"I will miss you, sir," Timothy said as we came up the steps. "But St. Louis isn't far away and I'll be home for holidays."

Grandfather patted his shoulder. "You're doing the best thing. No need to stay put when better chances present themselves."

I glanced at Andrew. He watched Timothy, his mouth pulled to one side, and he reached into his pocket for a cigarette.

"I'm so grateful for everything. For you coming to see me." Timothy turned to me. "And Annie, for you coming too." Suddenly he slapped his forehead. "I'll have to finish *Ivanhoe* by myself."

I nodded.

"Won't be as much fun, that's for sure."

The same feeling I had had the evening before suddenly swept over me. I wished that nothing would change, that I wouldn't have to go back to school, that Timothy could stay at St. John's, that Andrew and I could still have our afternoons to talk and read together. But then I realized that to wish that I would have to also hope that Timothy would stay blind and that Andrew's face would never

177

heal. Maybe I was just selfish. But I felt very sad and wondered how Timothy could be so happy. And Grandfather. Only Andrew seemed to share my mood.

"Well, I better move my old bones or they'll have to find a bed for me in here." Grandfather leaned heavily on Timothy as he stood up. "Now, you take care of yourself and write me a note or two. But not too many. You'll be busy getting on with life." Grandfather steadied himself on Timothy's arm and hugged him for a moment. "Good-bye, my boy. Don't walk us out. Annie will help me."

And he turned and walked steadily down the path away from the hospital. I turned to look. Timothy was standing on the porch with Andrew. I waved and Timothy blew me a kiss. Grandfather ignored Father, who wanted us to wait for Mother inside the hospital. I could tell that he wanted to leave St. John's. Maybe he felt the way I did about how everything was changing. So I helped him leave, helped him down the path, away from Timothy.

24

School started. And fall came. It came suddenly this year with a cold rain and days of wet and sogginess. The leaves hung on the trees in limp clusters. The summer that had brought so many changes to me was left behind with the blinding sun and the caroling of the cicadas. The men moved indoors, where they huddled around Victrolas and over checkers games on the dining-room tables. The trees around St. John's shadowed damp empty lawns.

The world around me was pulling itself back from the war. Newspapers carried fewer stories about Europe, as if to forget a place as well as a time. No one sang the war songs anymore, and we saw few men on the streets in uniform. The hospitals filled up with normal illnesses—old men like Grandfather with heart attacks, women having babies, children with broken legs and swollen tonsils.

But my family did not forget what the war had left us. Grandmother continued to live with the memory of Uncle Paul, the most real person in her life. Father continued his work at St. John's treating the young men who he said should have been out rowing on the lake instead of hobbling on shattered legs down long white corridors.

A week after Timothy left, Grandfather got a letter from him saying he'd found a job and talking about the pretty girls he saw on the streets of St. Louis. Grandfather immediately wrote back, telling Timothy about his tomatoes and squash and asking who he thought would win the

World Series. Grandfather still went out to St. John's. He'd found another man who liked to be read to, a man whose eyes would not get better, and so Grandfather cheerfully started *Ivanhoe* over again.

The first week in September, I started high school. I passed my old grammar school every day as I walked to the trolley stop and I watched the children playing on the grass in front, heard them screaming and laughing. I had been part of those games only a year before. One year ago, Uncle Paul had been dead only three months. Father was still in New York, the war was not yet over. And Andrew's face was still whole.

So much had changed in one year. Not only had I grown two inches and stopped wearing hair ribbons, but I had changed inside. One year ago, I believed my mother knew everything and that I would never have cause to disobey her. I knew my father could heal anyone and that my grandfather would live forever. And I thought Uncle Paul had died in glory.

One day Emily told me that high school scared her. I said that it did me too, but that wasn't the truth. What would I have to learn in high school that was harder than the truth of those words Eric Owen had whispered into that quiet room? And what would I have to face ever again that was more terrible than the pain in Andrew's eyes?

I had no classes with Emily and Darby this year and I seldom saw them. Things had changed. Emily seemed sillier to me than she had ever been before, laughing at nothing, noticing what I was wearing, pushing Fidelio away when he tried to kiss her as he always had before. Darby made one joke after another, taking nothing seriously, but laughing at everything and everyone around him. Still, they were my friends and I hoped that our friendship was just taking a holiday.

One day they caught up with me as I hurried to the trolley stop.

"Annie, come to the soda fountain with us," Emily said, panting. "We're meeting everyone."

"I'm sorry. I can't. I'm meeting someone."

"Anyone we know?" Darby asked.

"One of the patients at St. John's. A friend of mine."

"You mean the one with the face? The one you told us about?"

Earlier in the summer, I had mentioned Andrew to them, saying only that he'd been burned on his face.

"Yes, my friend Andrew."

Darby and Emily exchanged looks. I wished I hadn't said anything.

Emily wound her scarf tighter around her neck. "I'm sorry about what I said last summer. I guess you really like him, huh, Annie?"

I smiled at her. "I do. I wish you could meet Andrew."

She shifted her books. "No, I don't think so."

Darby flicked his book strap at a bush. "Why don't you just read *Frankenstein* instead?" He grinned at me.

"Darby!" Emily yelled.

He shrugged. "Just a joke."

Emily touched my arm. "I miss you, Annie. I wish we had classes together."

"Me too. But we see each other." I saw the trolley down the street.

"Not enough. Listen, let's go to the school party next week, OK?"

"OK." I nodded. The streetcar stopped and students started to climb on. "I have to go. 'Bye."

" 'Bye." Emily cupped her hands around her mouth. "Annie, don't be mad at Darby. He's just stupid."

I waved, but I didn't smile.

I didn't go to St. John's every day. I always checked with Andrew about his work schedule for the week and didn't go out on the days he was working in the wards. Often when I did go I found him playing checkers with the other men. He was always glad to see me and asked to see my books and about school. He laughed more than he had before and his good-bye wave was jaunty. In a way that I didn't understand and that made me ashamed, his happiness made me sad.

One Saturday morning in late September I was in my room reading when I heard the doorbell ring. I looked out the window and saw a truck in front of our house, a man sitting behind the wheel. Then I heard voices in the hall and Mother called my name.

I straightened my clothes and hair and hurried down. At the foot of the stairs standing beside Mother was Mrs. Crayton, Andrew's mother. I stopped, my breath in my mouth. Suddenly I was afraid. She had come to tell us bad news about him. But she reached out to take my hand and she was smiling.

"Annie, I'm so glad to see you again. And to meet your mother." She turned to Mother, who smiled back at her.

Mother said, "Please come in and sit down. My husband will be in soon. He's out back. Saturdays, you know. So many chores." She moved us both into the living room. "And your husband?" She paused as she reached for Mrs. Crayton's coat. "Won't he come in?"

"No, I can't stay long. I just wanted to stop by on our way home. I've, we've, that is, been to the hospital. And I brought you some of our apples. To thank you. They're on your porch." She waved absently toward the outside. "It's so little for all you've done."

I looked out the door and saw a box of red apples on top of the steps.

"Well, thank you." Mother nodded and folded her hands in her lap.

When my father came in, they all smiled again and we all sat down. Fidelio trotted in, greeted Mrs. Crayton, and lay at my feet. It began to rain.

Mrs. Crayton glanced outside. "I have to be getting on. Mr. Crayton hates to drive in the rain."

My parents nodded, but Andrew's mother didn't move from where she sat by my mother on the couch. She looked at all three of us in turn.

"You've done so much for Andrew, Dr. Metcalf. And you, Annie. It's hard. We live so far out and can get in so little, with the farm and all the work. Well, it made me feel better to know he had friends here. More than just the people at the hospital. And I want you to know that I thank you." She stopped and looked out at the rain a moment. "Andrew is, well, he's a good boy. It's hard to see him . . ."

Silence for a moment. Then Mother reached over and touched her arm. "I know."

Mrs. Crayton looked at her. "And it's more than the way he looks, his face and all. When he came back, he'd changed inside." She put her hand to her forehead. I noticed again how red her hand was. "I thought I was ready for it, I'd told myself he'd change. But it still seemed that the boy we sent away had died. Before, he was so full of life, so wanting to do things all the time. When he came back, he just sat." She pushed at her hair. No one else moved. Then she smiled at Father. "But he's so much better now, don't you think, Doctor?"

Father nodded.

"And I think a lot of that is thanks to you and Annie. Even helping him decide to . . . Oh, wait. I almost forgot. I brought something else to give you, Annie."

She picked up her purse from the floor beside her, reached in and handed something to me. "I thought you'd like to keep this."

It was a photograph of a young man standing against a background of trees, sun bright on his face and full in his eyes. He didn't squint or frown, just looked at the camera, hands behind his back, wisps of light hair brushing his forehead. All this I saw in one moment. A picture of a stranger. Why had Mrs. Crayton given . . .

His face. I looked again. Freckles drifted across the nose, the mouth almost smiled, a smile that would crease the smooth cheeks.

I lifted my head. Mrs. Crayton clutched a handkerchief in her hand.

"His sister took it just before he left. It's one of the few pictures we have of him before . . ."

I looked down at the photograph. Before the gas burned off the freckles and ate away the lips and singed the cheeks.

Andrew. This was his face. The moment before the gas covered him, he looked like this.

I turned the photograph facedown in my lap and covered it with my hand.

"Thank you, Mrs. Crayton." I wished I had never seen this photograph.

"Well, it's the least I could do. After all you've done for him." She shook her head. "He will surely miss you."

The rain poured down the window behind her. Mother and Father both turned to look at me and Father began to get out of his chair.

They all seemed to be waiting for me to say something.

I stared at Andrew's mother. "What do you mean?"

"Annie, it's just been decided," Father said. "I was going to tell you."

Mother interrupted him. "Annie, dear . . ."

"Oh, I'm so sorry. She doesn't know? I thought . . ."

"Know what? Where is Andrew going?" I stood up and looked at them where they all sat looking at me. "Tell me."

Father looked down at me. "He's decided to take a job at a hospital in Topeka. He'll be trained to work with wounded men, the kind of work he's been doing here, only it will be a real job. He'll be trained, he'll be paid. He can be independent. So he decided—"

"He decided? He doesn't have to? You didn't tell him he has to leave?"

"We never decide things like that for patients. It has to be his decision."

"He *wants* to go?"

"Yes, Annie." Father put his hand on my arm.

I pulled away, turned and ran out of the house, slamming the door behind me. I ran down the steps, past the apples now spattered with rain. I didn't look at Andrew's father sitting in the truck, but ran past him and down the street. Andrew had to change his mind. I had to make him stay.

25

The rain misted about me as I ran. I ran three blocks before I had to stop, out of breath. I sat for a moment on a low wall, breathing hard, and pushed my hair out of my eyes. The rain had stopped, but now it seemed colder. How far still to the hospital? I wasn't sure. The streetcar took a different route. I got up and began to walk.

I had gone another block when a car pulled up to the curb beside me. I glanced at it and kept walking. The car kept pace with me.

"Annie." Mother's voice. "Annie, get in."

"No!"

"Annie, get in the car. I'll take you to Andrew."

I turned and looked at her. She nodded and beckoned to me. "Get in. It's cold and you're wet."

I climbed into the car and she handed me a sweater and a towel. "Get dry before we get there. Andrew doesn't want to see you like this."

I leaned against the door, the sweater pulled around me. Neither of us spoke. The rain began again. Mother pulled up the long drive to St. John's and stopped at the steps to the front door. "Do you want me to go in with you?" she asked.

I shook my head. I turned to look up the steps.

She reached across and covered my hands with hers. "Try to understand, Annie. Try to understand for his sake."

I pressed my lips together and turned away. She sighed and gave my hands a final squeeze. "Your father will come in about an hour to get you."

I nodded and got out of the car. I climbed the steps to St. John's and opened the heavy wooden door.

I found Andrew in the dining room playing checkers with another patient. The other man saw me first and spoke quietly to Andrew, who turned and then hurried to me where I stood in the door.

"Annie! What—?"

"I have to talk to you."

"You're all wet. Your hair!" He reached out and touched the top of my head. "What have you been doing?"

"Your mother came to see us."

"I know. She just left here. She said she was going to stop on her way home."

"And she told me you're leaving." On the last word I began to cry, sobbing helplessly into my hands.

"Oh, Annie." He reached out to me but I backed away. "I wanted to tell you myself."

"Tell me what? That you want to go away?"

"Here, Annie." He handed me a napkin from the table. "Here, wipe your face and sit down." He pushed the checkerboard aside. The other man had left.

"I don't want to sit down! Stop treating me like a child!"

"Annie, sit down. I'm not treating you like a child. I just want to explain. Give me a chance." He rubbed his hair with his hand. "You scared me to death coming in here like that. I thought something terrible had happened."

"Something has. You're going away. And you don't have to." I sat down next to him.

"Yes, I do. I have to do this."

"No, Father said not. He said *you* decided to go to Topeka."

"That's right. I decided." He reached out to me and took both my hands. "I decided and that's important. I

187

haven't decided anything for myself in a long time. Things have just happened to me. Ever since I've been here I've been taken care of, things done for me, decisions made for me." He shook my hands a little and leaned toward me. "Ever since I was wounded. Ever since I joined the army. No decisions. Just do what I'm told. Do you know how helpless that makes me feel?"

"You're not helpless. That's silly. That's no reason—"

"No? How many times have you told me how mad you get when your mother tells you what to do? When she makes your decisions for you? You always say she makes you feel like a child, don't you?"

"That's not the same. You—"

"And what did you do when you were told not to come see me again?" He leaned back against the table and waved his hand. "You came anyway. Decided for yourself what was right for you." He leaned forward and looked into my face. "That's what being an adult is—making decisions for yourself. And that's what I haven't done for a long time. Do you understand?"

I shrugged my shoulders and drew circles on the table with a finger. I didn't *want* to understand. I shivered a little.

"Here, wait a minute." He got up and left and I sat. I didn't feel like crying anymore. I just felt tired. Then Andrew was back, draping a blanket over my shoulders. It felt warm and I huddled inside it.

"I should have done this before. You'll get sick." He sat down again. "You know, Annie, this is really all your fault." He was smiling.

I sat up straight and glared at him. "What do you mean? I never . . . !"

He put his hand over my mouth, his fingers warm on my cold skin.

"I've learned from you, Annie. You made me get going again. With your talk of going off to Egypt. The way you kept asking about your uncle. You don't just sit and let things happen to you. Before I met you, I just sat around feeling sorry for myself. You know how I was. Mean to you, always angry, keeping away from everyone. Because . . . I knew what I looked like and I knew people were scared of me."

"I was scared of you," I said quietly.

"I know." I looked up at him. "You sure looked scared. But you came back, remember? And you talked to me, reminded me that I wasn't the only one the war had hurt. Although why I needed to be reminded of that, living here—" He shook his head. "The night we found out about your uncle, I did a lot of thinking. I always thought I'd been unlucky, getting caught like I did. But to die of measles . . ." He shook his head again and looked down at the table. "That's so much worse," he said quietly.

I thought of the thinking I had done that same night.

"So, Annie," he said, "you made me get off my duff and take over my life again. And see that others had it worse. You're pretty great."

I shook my head. "No, I'm not."

He pulled the blanket tighter around me. "Yes, you are. Paul and I couldn't both be wrong."

I looked away, my eyes filling with tears. "Then why do you have to leave me, too?"

"Listen to me. I have to think about the future. I can't stay here forever. I've got to find a way to earn a living, to take care of myself. And not many places would hire me, looking like I do. So when your dad came up with this idea—"

"My father? He got the job for you?"

He looked at me a moment without speaking. Then he nodded. "Yes, he did."

I turned away.

"But I'd asked him what I should do. He said he'd think about it. A friend of his in Topeka told him about this job and he thought of me. I was going to tell you when . . . I thought I could." He whispered the last words.

I stood up and walked to the tall windows and watched the sheets of rain coat the glass and dim everything outside. "Last summer, your mother told me . . ." I turned and looked at Andrew. "She said you enlisted. That you weren't drafted. You didn't have to be in the army. You didn't have to go. And look what happened."

Andrew sat where I'd left him, his bandaged hand cradled in his lap, his head resting on his good hand. In the dimming light of the huge echoing room, he looked very tired.

"You didn't have to go then. You don't have to go now."

He looked up at me and then back down at the table. "I know how it must seem to you." He shook his head. "I thought then I was doing the right thing. I don't know now. That was a long time ago." He paused and took a long breath. "And maybe this time won't be any better. Maybe I'm making the wrong decision again." He looked at me. "But I have to keep trying, don't I?"

I looked out the window. I heard him sigh and I turned. As I leaned against the wall I watched him where he sat, alone. He looked like all the other men in the hospital, his face empty, his hands still. Lately, he'd been so cheerful. Just a minute ago, he'd been smiling. Now, when my back was turned, when he thought I wasn't watching him, he looked like an old man. Like the men who sat, day after day, and looked at us.

190

"Andrew." He looked up at me. "I'm tired and you look . . ." I paused. "You look tired too. Let's not talk about this anymore right now."

"OK." He nodded. "Anyway, I'm not leaving right away. We still have time."

"OK, we'll talk about it again."

He nodded his head to the checkerboard. "Want a game?"

He let me win, and when I yelled at him, he grinned and said he'd done it to cheer me up. It did, so that by the time Father came to take me home, I could say good-bye to Andrew without crying like a child.

26

I did not cry, but on the drive home I was miserable. I knew that now I would start counting down the days we had together, finding this and that thing we were doing for the last time, just as I always did before every birthday. This is the last dinner I'll eat when I'm ten, or this is the last walk I'll take to school when I'm twelve. Only now, each last thing would be surrounded with pain so sharp that it would make me cry. Was this the last time Andrew and I would ever play checkers together on a rainy afternoon?

When I went up to my room to get ready for dinner, I found the picture of Andrew lying on my dresser. Father, or maybe Mother, had put it there after I ran out into the rain. I picked it up and looked at it again. Nothing in the picture looked like Andrew. This face that no one would particularly notice, that would frighten no one, didn't look like Andrew. I wondered if he remembered what he had once looked like.

I picked up the other photograph that stood on the dresser.

"Andrew said you were unlucky to die of measles," I whispered to Uncle Paul. Then I caught a shaking breath. "I wish you were here, too. Even if . . ." I looked at Paul's bright face. "Even if you looked like Andrew." My hand rested for a moment across his face before I returned the picture to its spot in front of the mirror.

I stood a moment more and then propped the picture

of Andrew against my china bank, just to the right of Paul.

That night at dinner, Father talked about Andrew.

"He's right to do this, Annie. To look to his future."

"Couldn't he stay with his family?" Mother asked quietly. "His mother seemed very nice."

"I gather there's a problem with his father. He's not very accepting of Andrew's . . . condition." Father spoke slowly, as if being careful of each word.

"Oh." Mother played with her silverware.

"I think he's cruel, don't you, Father? Andrew could stay in Kansas City then. He wouldn't have to go so far away." I didn't look at Mother.

"Andrew's not going to have an easy time, that's for sure. It took courage for him to make this first move. To leave St. John's, where things are easy for him."

"Could he stay at St. John's if he wanted to?"

"You mean forever?"

I paused a moment before I said, "Yes."

"Would you want him to?"

I looked at them both and then out the window at the darkness. I shook my head slowly. "I don't know."

Mother cleared her throat. "Well, I'd like to make a suggestion. I think we should invite Andrew to dinner."

Father and I both stared at her.

She laughed a little and cocked her head. "Don't look so shocked, you two. I know I haven't been very much help with all this. But I can change too." Her voice shook a little as she said the last words.

"Katherine, what a wonderful idea. Let's do it. What do you say, Annie?"

I couldn't speak for a minute. I was mixed with joy and

fear. To have Andrew here, in my house, sitting in one of our chairs, seeing Fidelio!

"Maybe you could prepare dinner, Annie. That ham loaf I taught you to fix. I'll help, of course, but I think Andrew would enjoy it more knowing you were the cook."

Mother's voice carried the calm, sure tone she always used when planning a party, something she did with ease and style. The thought of fixing dinner terrified me. And for Andrew! I tried to imagine him at our table, eating food I'd cooked.

Mother was watching me, a tiny frown gathering in her eyes. I got up and wrapped my arms around her. "Thank you, Mother. I know he'll come. It's a wonderful idea."

"How about next Friday?" Father nodded. None of us had to be reminded that it had to be soon. "Maybe you could invite Ruth. She's heard so much about Andrew."

When I asked Andrew the next day, he lifted his head and frowned at me for a moment.

"Dinner? At your house? Is your mom gone again?"

"No, it was her idea. Honest."

He shook his head. "Doesn't make sense."

"She's changed. I think she's really trying. Ever since we found out about Paul." And since I said those things to her, I thought to myself. "You want to come?"

"Sure. I haven't been in a house for, oh, a long time. I may forget how to act. Sit on the dog or something."

"Oh, Andrew. I was worried that you wouldn't want to."

"No, I want to, very much. Thank your mom for me. That's very nice of her."

Ruth wasn't at home when I called, so after school on Tuesday I went to the library to invite her. When I asked for Ruth, Miss Crenshaw, the librarian who always helped me find books, but who was a bit stern, said, "*Miss Sylvester* is sorting books. In the *basement*." Then she smiled. "Of all places."

I found Ruth surrounded by piles of books, checking titles against a list on the table in front of her. When I told her about Mother's idea, she clapped shut the book in her hand and gave its cover a sharp tap. "Oh, good for her. Good, good for her."

"It's just dinner."

"No, it's not. It's much more. This means your mother is finally accepting everything that's happened. Beginning with Paul's death."

I straightened the stack of books in front of me. "Did she tell you about that?"

"Yes, all about it." She checked off the book in her hand and set it on top of the stack. Then she sat back on her stool and crossed her arms. "She also told me about the talk you two had."

I brushed my hair back. My cheeks felt hot. "Did she seem upset about it?"

"Upset, yes. But not at you. She's proud of you, Annie. You have more sense now than some people have at age eighty." She thumped her fist on the books in front of her. "Don't get me started." She opened another book and stared at the page. Then she closed it again.

"But Mother *was* upset about Uncle Paul."

"Yes. Of course, from the very beginning she didn't want him to go. She wouldn't even go to the station to see him off. This just makes it harder."

"Ruth, there's something I don't understand. Andrew's mother told me he wasn't drafted. He enlisted in the army."

"So did Paul."

195

"Yes." I paused, swallowing hard. "Why would they want to go, when it all turned out so—terribly?"

"Because they didn't know. Young men like Andrew, all they heard was how glorious the war would be. They could all be heroes. Don't you remember the big parade down to the station when the first unit left? Bands, speeches, flowers in their buttonholes." She paused and shook her head. "That's hard to resist. They didn't know about anything else."

"Didn't anybody know?"

"Oh, a few people said we shouldn't get into the war. Not too many around here. And it wasn't a very popular idea."

"Did you feel that way?"

"Yes."

"Did you talk to Uncle Paul?"

"Yes. But he didn't listen. He just laughed at your mother and me, told us not to worry, said he'd be fine. All the usual things."

I thought of all the things he'd said he wanted to do in his life.

Ruth stared at the ceiling above us. "And it could all start again."

"What do you mean?"

She let out a gust of air. "In this morning's paper there's an article about an American army that has been fighting in Russia." She looked at me. "And St. John's is still full of casualties from the last war."

"More fighting?"

"Always more. Doesn't it seem insane to you? I wonder sometimes if I'm the only one who feels this way. It just seems so wrong and yet we keep doing it. Maybe I just don't understand enough about the realities of the world."

She riffled the pages of the book in front of her. "I guess I just don't understand."

I'd never seen Ruth so troubled. She was always calm, sure, so able to help me understand things.

"Annie, one thing. Don't let this change the way you feel about Paul. Just remember him for the wonderful person we all loved. He did what he thought was right. And he did it courageously as long as he could. That is what you should remember. Not the waste of his death."

"Andrew said that too. That he thought he was doing the right thing when he enlisted, but now he's not sure."

"Well, yes, I can see why. Glorious war must be a hard thing for him to believe in now."

"I wish it all wasn't so confusing. Ever since Father came home, I've felt jumbled up. Like . . . like a big eggbeater mixed me all up inside."

Ruth laughed. "Exactly the way to be. That means you're thinking. You haven't got the truth all figured out. You're still discovering it." She paused. "So is your mother."

"Then it doesn't get easier?"

"It shouldn't." She rested one hand on my arm and with the other she gently touched my face. "I told you not to let me get started. I always have to remind myself how very painful it is to question the war. It's so much easier to put it away in memories and not to think. That's why people aren't very understanding, why they can't be more generous to Andrew and the others at St. John's. So don't be too hard on them. Everyone doesn't have your strength. Just keep your own eyes clear and wide open. That's the most important thing." She hugged me to her for one moment and then went back to her stack of books. As I picked up my books from the floor and turned to leave, she began to laugh. "I almost forgot. Yes, I'd love to come to your dinner party. I'm anxious to meet Andrew. I'll bring dessert. We'll have a splendid time."

I hoped Ruth was right, but I lived in agony for the rest of the week. I lay awake late every night, but not worrying about how to cook ham and green beans. It was the memory of the only other time Mother and Andrew had met and the fear that some shadow of that day would spoil the evening.

But I underestimated everyone. When I heard the car in the driveway, I looked at Mother in panic. But she just patted her hair, tucked her arm through Ruth's and said, "Annie, let's go greet your guest."

Andrew was dressed in his uniform. He even had his cap on, sitting on the back of his head. From a distance, he looked like any other soldier. Fidelio bounded around from the back, up to Father who ruffled his face and around the car to Andrew. Andrew let him lick his good hand, holding the bandaged hand away from the dog. I watched from the porch.

Father waved to me. "Hi, Annie."

I waved back. Andrew looked up at me and then stood up straight and saluted me.

He seemed a stranger, until he and Father came around the bushes and up the steps and it was my Andrew, now that I could see his face. His eyes were bright even in the shadows of the porch and his mouth was stretched in what I had come to know was his widest smile.

"Hello, Annie." But as he spoke, Andrew looked behind me to where my mother stood.

I turned. "Mother, this is Andrew." Of course she knew that. But no one was even looking at me.

"Hello, Andrew. I'm so glad you could come." She held out her hand. Andrew reached out to her and she gently took his hand in hers. Even though I had thought about this moment for months, even though I knew it would happen, I still looked at my mother in astonishment. Andrew was here. My mother was looking at him. Steadily, quietly, as graciously as she greeted friends at church, she welcomed Andrew into our home. Then I introduced him to Ruth. And inside I felt that I might explode with happiness.

Everything *was* splendid. I couldn't eat much, but everyone else said the food was good. I didn't drop anything, and the one time that Andrew's fork slipped out of his hand and clattered to the floor, he picked it up and no one seemed to notice.

After dinner, as the adults sat over coffee, the curtains blew in around Andrew where he sat and the cool of early autumn came into the room. Ruth and Father were talking about the situation in Germany and I looked at Andrew as he rested his cheek on his hand and stirred his coffee. I had trouble realizing that we had not sat like this before. I wanted him to stay, to go upstairs and sleep in the spare room and never leave. He belonged here with all of us who cared about him.

I turned and saw Mother looking at him too, and a moment later as she moved behind him to pull back the curtain, she rested her hand on his shoulder.

Before he left, Andrew asked Mother if she would play the piano since he'd heard so much about her music from me. So we all went into the living room. She didn't play long, but Andrew put his head back against the couch and watched her, smiling, his hand in its bandages moving to the rhythm. When she played the last chord and turned on the piano bench to face us, he clapped gently and stood up.

199

"Mrs. Metcalf, would you come out to St. John's and give a concert for the men? I can't tell you how much they'd love it."

Mother sat without moving. I glanced at Ruth and saw she was watching Mother.

"November eleventh would be a good day. That's the anniversary of the end of the war."

Mother nodded. "One year ago." She looked at him, still not moving.

"Would you? At least think about coming."

Suddenly Mother stood up and closed the lid of the piano. "Yes, I will." She lifted her chin a little and looked at Father and then back at Andrew. "I will do it for you, Andrew. And that day would be most appropriate."

"Thank you. I really appreciate it, ma'am."

Then Father said he'd get the car started. Ruth shook hands with Andrew and said she'd look forward to seeing him again.

Mother looked up at him and smiled. "I'm glad I had the chance to meet you, Andrew. I'm sorry it's taken me so long to learn the truth. About so much."

Andrew turned to me. "Annie, will you come out to the car with me?"

We stood on the porch for a minute, watching Father puttering over the car. Andrew turned to look down at me. "I wanted to tell you this time in the right way, Annie. I'll be leaving on November twelfth. The day after the concert."

He'd only be here three more weeks. Now I knew.

"Tonight was wonderful. You always seem to know just what I need. Thank you for inviting me."

I watched as he ran out to the car, watched the head-lights back down the drive and saw him wave from the window. The evening was over.

27

The middle of October and the weather turned even colder. I walked to the trolley through cool yellow days and slept under two blankets through the cold nights.

I had to learn to live my life without Andrew, to make the space he took up in my life smaller so his going would not leave such a gaping hole. As days passed, I looked around at the other men in the hospital, trying to imagine seeing only them, without Andrew nearby. But everything I did only made me realize how hard it was going to be, how much I would miss my friend.

Another celebration was planned for November eleventh. One morning at breakfast, Mother folded the newspaper in half and said, "Listen."

Father put down his coffee cup.

" 'Plans for the War Memorial Proceed,' " she read. " 'The Reverend Dr. Bingham of Valley Presbyterian Church and Father Moncrief of St. Mary's Catholic Church announced today that five thousand dollars has been raised for the memorial to those who died in the Great War and that the drawing of the memorial has been completed. The public is invited to view the plans on display in the library.' " Mother looked at Father. "Then the article lists all the men from this area who were killed or are missing and asks all relatives to check that their dead or missing are included and"—Mother began to laugh—"that all names are spelled correctly."

"Is Uncle Paul there?" I leaned over her shoulder.

"Hmmm, let's see." She ran her finger down the list. "Yes, here it is. Paul Robert MacLeod."

It was spelled right. So Uncle Paul would be on the memorial. No matter how he died.

"There's more." Mother took a sip of her coffee and read on. " 'The church leaders announced that a ceremony is being planned for the first anniversary of the end of the war to be held on the spot where the monument will be placed. Mayor Evans, U.S. Representative Hanson, and representatives of the army and navy will be present. The public is invited.' " Mother threw the paper down. "Quite a celebration. Well, they can celebrate without me."

Father just nodded and finished his coffee.

I read the rest of the article myself and later I told Andrew about the ceremony. He listened while I told him about the parade before the ceremony, about the troops that were to be honor guards, the bands that were to play, the speeches by the mayor and the congressman. The article had also said that the schoolchildren were to sing patriotic songs.

He listened, moving the checkers about the board. His right arm had become infected and so was rebandaged up to the elbow. Only his hand was free, and he now wore shirts with both sleeves cut off. He listened and then said, "I wonder why we weren't invited?"

"But it said there'll be an honor guard."

"Yes, but it won't have anyone from St. John's in it. Bet on that."

"Well, who will be the honor guard?"

"Oh, veterans, the ones who came back in good shape. Don't worry, Annie. I don't think the guys out here would go even if they were asked. Memorials . . ." He waved the newly bandaged arm. "Better to buy us all a good cigar. Don't even think about it."

But I couldn't help thinking about it. Everyone in town seemed to think the ceremony was a splendid idea. My friends at school talked about it constantly. My grandmother planned to go to see Paul's name on the monument. The hospital was the only place where the big day wasn't on everyone's mind.

At school we began to practice our songs. Miss Marshall, the music teacher, took command and pulled us from our studies without asking permission of our regular teachers. Whenever she appeared at the classroom door with stacks of music in her hand, we put away our other books and went. No one said a word.

I hated every note of music we sang. Here I couldn't get away with mouthing the words because Miss Marshall prowled among us, bending low to hear our voices, her short bobbed hair swinging in our faces to the rhythm of the music.

Andrew wasn't invited, Andrew and all the others who most deserved to be there. Uncle Paul's name on the monument would be a lie. If people knew how he'd died, they wouldn't for one minute let his name remain with those of the others. Paul Robert MacLeod would be chiseled away.

As I stood among my friends, the tune "Onward, Christian Soldiers" swirling around me, I knew I couldn't go to the ceremony. Everything that had happened since I had looked into that man's face at the train station last spring told me I couldn't go. If Andrew hadn't been invited and Uncle Paul didn't belong there, then neither did I. The ceremony was for those like my grandmother, those who still believed.

28

Andrew was leaving. Five days, four. Three. Now it was only two days away.

The day before the ceremony, we were released from school an hour early to go home and rest. I was glad to be away from it all. When I got home, I found a note from Mother saying she'd be back around five and asking me to take a magazine across to Grandmother.

As I crossed the street, I heard pounding from the backyard. Grandfather stood in the middle of a pile of wood, feeble afternoon sun all around him.

"Hiya, Annie." He waved.

"Hi, Grandfather. What are you making?"

"Oh"—he waved at the mess around him—"I thought I'd prop up the tool shed a bit. It's real wobbly. Probably because that dog of yours"—now he waved at Fidelio, who panted at my heels—"thinks it's his to sleep on."

We both turned to look at the shed. It was leaning to the left against the fence.

"Paul made that. The summer after high school. Handy boy with a hammer." He began to pound again.

"Paul?" I dropped my bookbag on a board and sat down beside it. "I didn't know Uncle Paul liked to make things."

Grandfather stopped working. "Sure he did. Why, he was handy about the house. Repaired a lot for your dad." He set the hammer down and sat across from me. He took out a handkerchief and wiped his face. "He was especially good with wood. He loved to feel a smooth, cool piece of wood."

Grandfather smoothed the board he sat on with the handkerchief.

He chuckled suddenly. "Do you know how much Paul would have hated tomorrow? He always made fun of parades and bands and speeches. Thought they were a grand waste of time. And now, one is to be held in his honor. How he'd laugh." He chuckled again.

"Now mind me, Annie. Don't tell your grandmother I said that. Tomorrow is a sacred thing for her. She wouldn't want to know I'd been laughing about Paul." He paused a moment. "Some things she's better off not knowing."

I looked up at him. He nodded slowly. "Better off."

So he knew.

He turned to look at the shed again. "I wish he was here to help me fix the shed. He was so good with wood."

"You must miss him a lot."

He turned to me again. "He's gone—I can accept that, and I'll go on without him. I'll miss him every day I have left to live, but I'll not give up the rest of my life for him, as your grandmother is doing. That does him no good."

He shook his head. "No good. You remember that, Annie. Don't go living your life around Andrew and wasting your young life. He loves you because you are living and whole and happy." He put his arm around me and we stood in the darkening afternoon, the cold air pushing us together.

"I'm not going to sing in the ceremony with my class," I said. "I don't want to be part of it."

"You're not?"

I shook my head. "No." I looked up at him. "Do you mind?"

"No. I wish I didn't have to."

"Andrew said they'd do better to buy all the men at St. John's a good cigar."

Grandfather chuckled and then put his head back and laughed out loud. I could feel his body shake against mine. "How true. How true." He wiped his face with his hand. "Well, it makes people in town feel good about all that has happened." We stood silent for several minutes. It was almost dark now.

"But maybe that's not such a good thing," I said passionately. "Maybe they should never feel good about all that. Never feel good and never forget. That's why I wish some of the men at St. John's were going to be there tomorrow. Just to remind them."

Grandfather hugged me to him and held me as he spoke. "We're a lucky family, Annie. We lost Paul, but we've got you and John and your cousins." He pulled me closer to him and we stood quietly for a moment in the dark yard.

"Well, your grandmother would be furious to find me out here. You scoot home and I'll see you early tomorrow."

Mother was home when I got there. She turned from the stove as I came in. "Hi, Annie." She smoothed back my hair. "How was school?"

"Fine." I smiled up at her. "Are you ready for tomorrow?"

"I think so. I better be. Are you?"

"Almost. I've got to phone Andrew. I think . . . maybe I'll go to the ceremony tomorrow after all. If he'll go with me."

She raised her eyebrows and clucked a bit. "Well, won't that be interesting?"

It took several minutes for Sister Gretchen to find Andrew. I'd never called him before, but I was ready to insist if they wouldn't let me talk to him. But soon he was there.

"Annie, hello." Again, his voice sounded deeper over the phone.

"Hi, Andrew. Listen, I have a plan. Are you busy to-morrow?"

"Well, the concert—"

"No, I mean in the morning. You want to go to the ceremony with me? For the monument?"

I heard nothing for a long moment.

Finally he said, "Aren't you singing?"

"No, I'm not. I want to be there with you."

"Oh, Annie." Silence again. I stared at the floor. I could see him, alone in the hall, leaning against the wall, holding the phone with his bandaged hand.

Finally I heard him say, "OK."

"You're sure?" Had I asked too much?

"Sure. You want me to meet you there?"

"Yes. It starts at nine, sharp."

"Fine, I'll be there." Another silence. "Good night, Annie."

"Good night, Andrew."

29

Next morning, the sun was bright with the pale yellow of fall. The bare trees and dull-brown ground looked warmer than they had for weeks. As I walked to the park with my grandparents, I let my coat swing open. I could almost imagine it was spring. They found seats along the street, near the roped-off slab of concrete where the ceremony was to be held. Grandfather hadn't seemed surprised when I told him I would be at the ceremony after all. And when I said Andrew was coming, he'd said, "Good for him."

Yesterday at school, I had told Miss Marshall that I wouldn't be singing with the others. I was ready to tell her why, but I didn't have to. She nodded, pressed her lips together and said, "If that's your decision."

I stood at the back of the crowd, watching my friends file into the risers that stood to one side of the speaker's platform. I didn't want to talk to any of them today, because they would ask questions and make comments.

I also stayed away from everyone else to watch for Andrew. I knew that what I had asked him to do would be hard. He hadn't left St. John's except to come to our house for dinner. And I was sure that many of those in the crowd in front of me would stare at him.

Everyone was dressed up, with bright ribbons in hats and women's hair. A man was selling balloons and the bright colors added to the summer-carnival feeling. I could hear the band warming up behind the risers. Men in long dark coats stood in groups in front of the speaker's stand.

Other men in uniforms covered with ribbons gathered under the trees and smoked cigarettes. Everyone was waiting for the parade to begin.

Suddenly I thought of the train station. I saw again the lines of men in uniform jumping off the train and running to their families. Maybe some of those men now stood in the shadows. But the men in wheelchairs and on stretchers were not here today. They were not here to hear the bands and the speeches. They would never be in a parade again.

I glanced at the concrete slab in front of the speaker's platform. To the side was a drawing of the monument and a list of the names of the dead.

Those men were not here today either. And the happy crowd in front of me was not thinking of them. Then I looked for my grandparents. They were thinking today of Paul, I was sure. Grandmother had showed me his picture tucked inside her purse. One dead man was being remembered today. Maybe among the crowd laughing in front of me there were others.

I felt someone behind me. I turned. Andrew. He wore a slouch hat, goggles and a white scarf tied around his neck.

"Hi, Andrew."

"I was afraid I'd be late." He pulled the goggles off and unwound the scarf from around his face. Then he said, "There." He stood in the shadow of the tree, straight, like a soldier at attention. Anyone in the crowd who turned around could have seen his reddened skin, his slit of a mouth, his misshapen nose.

"No," I said, "you're just in time."

Just then I heard the brass band from the street and saw the tips of the flags over the heads of the crowd. The parade had begun.

209

I saw the rest of the day through Andrew's eyes and heard the music through his ears. The choir sang well, Miss Marshall bobbing and weaving in front of them. They sang "Columbia, the Gem of the Ocean," "Onward, Christian Soldiers," and a medley of songs from the war, those songs Mother wouldn't let me sing.

Then the mayor rose to speak.

"One year ago today, we here at home heard the joyous news of armistice. The long nightmare was at an end. Once the guns spoke no more, our soldiers and sailors would soon return and freedom would spread its wings across lands that had long suffered under autocracy. All sorrows and cares were thrown aside as joy filled every bosom."

Andrew crossed his arms. I leaned back against the tree.

"But in many homes, sorrow would not be banished and joy could find no place. Those loving hearts who had seen their dear ones depart forever, who knew the stilling of the guns had come too late, for them November eleventh must have seemed a bitter mockery."

I glanced up at Andrew. Bitter for him, too. The armistice had come a month too late for him.

"Today, in our meager way, we seek to soften that sad memory, by reassuring the families of those brave men who died the death of heroes that their names are carved forever in our hearts, that we shall never forget their sacrifice.

"Today we dedicate this monument that the names of those dear ones will be before our eyes as we go about our daily lives and so that their sacrifice will be an inspiration to us, a symbol of the true meaning of patriotism. May their families now find a softening of their sorrow in this day, as November eleventh takes on new meaning,

210

the day their loss becomes our own, and our pride in these brave men burnishes their memory to richest gold. We will never forget them. For now, they live among the angels."

Around us, the crowd applauded and cheered and the mayor bowed his head. The clapping continued and, as it did, I reached out and took Andrew's hand and held it in both of mine.

Then the songs, the band music and the speeches were over. The time came for the minister to read the names of the dead and missing, among them that of my uncle, Paul Robert MacLeod. There was no sound from the crowd and many people bowed their heads under the weight of the morning sun. The list was not long, but Reverend Bingham read slowly, pausing after each name so it was long before he finished. As he ended, the crowd seemed to give one long sigh. Beside me, Andrew stared straight ahead. A group of soldiers stood at attention at one side of the platform. When the minister folded the paper and sat down, the men in uniform slowly saluted.

Then it was over. In the rush, I found my grandparents and told them I was going to go home with a friend. Grandfather nodded and smiled and said, "Enjoy yourself, Annie." Grandmother was crying. When I pushed back through the crowd to Andrew, he was standing in the street beside the motorcycle, a cigarette in his hand. I stood on the grass, staring openmouthed at him.

"Want a ride? I have it for the whole day."

"Really? You came on it?"

"Sure. Your dad arranged it. Come on. Or are you afraid to ride with me?"

"Of course not. You're as good on it as Uncle Paul was."

So once again I climbed on the back of the motorcycle,

perched my shoes on the footrests and held on to the man in front of me.

Andrew backed out carefully, then stopped to wind the white scarf around his mouth and throat. I helped him tuck it under so it would not whip my face. I held my hat in front of me and buttoned my jacket up in front against the chilly wind.

Even if I see France and Egypt and the Yangtze, and all the other places on my maps, I will never forget that ride with Andrew across the lean November day. We stopped frequently so that Andrew could rest, but we didn't speak much. I wanted to tell him again that I was sorry for so many things—for not understanding why he was leaving, for running away that first day.

I also wanted somehow to tell him how this was a summer unlike any other I had ever lived, that while I had learned that love was not enough, that it did not make the sun rise in the morning and did not always shelter those in its circle, that I had learned other things too. And the learning had begun when I first saw Andrew's face.

But I didn't say these things.

And then it was evening and time for the concert. As my parents and I stood in the doorway of the hospital dining room, we saw the men, arranged in long curving rows, their wheelchairs, stretchers and chairs arching around the room. At the end of the room, under the tall windows, stood a grand piano, its lid propped open, looking like a great black swan ruffling its wings. Men talked quietly. The still hospital air hummed with the excitement I remembered from the opera house the night Uncle Paul and I had seen *La Bohème*.

Mother stood for a moment looking at the men. Father watched her, his hand on the doorknob. After a moment she glanced down at the music in her arms, looked at him and said, "Well, no turning back now. It looks like we're expected." And she walked up the aisle to the piano.

Father followed her. As I stood watching them, I heard my name. It was Andrew dressed in his uniform.

"Quite an evening. We should have sold tickets."

"You look elegant. I like your uniform."

"Real fancy, huh? You look swell too."

I looked at the other men, most of them wearing uniforms or parts of uniforms. Some had medals pinned to their jackets or bathrobes.

"Where's your Purple Heart, Andrew?"

He shrugged. "I don't like to wear it. I may take it out to my parents. After I get settled in my job, I'm going out there. I'm going to talk to my dad . . . well, try to talk to him. See if he won't . . ." He paused. "See if we can't try to get along again."

"Then you'll come back?"

"Sure. Topeka is only sixty miles away. It's not like I'm sailing off to India, or France."

"You promise?"

"Yes, I promise." He put his hand over his heart. Then he said, "Look at your mother."

And we both looked at the room filling up with men and at my mother, standing at the piano, surrounded by men in wheelchairs and on crutches.

"Who would have thought?" murmured Andrew.

Mother played all the pieces she loved—Chopin, Mozart, Brahms and Schumann. The sounds from the piano moved out through the room, reaching down to the men on the stretchers, wrapping around the nuns standing behind the wheelchairs, disappearing into the darkness around us.

We were wrapped in music and the heavy warmth of

the room—nuns, patients, Andrew, Father and I. The silence around the edges of the music deepened and darkened. I was no longer conscious of the music, just the sound that held me.

No one mentioned the anniversary, no one made speeches. The music ended and the men sat quietly and there were a few scatters of applause. Then one of the nuns rose and thanked Mother for playing and one of the patients handed her a bundle of roses. Mother smiled and pushed at her hair.

The men began to leave and I knew that the good-byes for my family and for Andrew would begin now. Father and I were going to see him off at the station in the morning, but Mother was not coming with us. Once one of us said good-bye to him, there would be no way to pretend he wasn't really leaving.

But Mother made it easy. She began to talk about how soon he would have time off so that he could come visit, she talked about getting together with his mother, she fussed with her music and asked him to carry the roses. We all walked out the front door and to our car.

I almost didn't notice when Mother finally turned to Andrew, looked at him a long moment and then said, "Good-bye, my dear."

30

Father and I stood waiting on the train platform as the train going west filled with luggage and mail and chattering passengers with tickets for California. It was early, but the depot was busy. We stood to the side, waiting for the ambulance that would bring Andrew and the other patients who were going to the hospital in Topeka.

Father kept his hand on my shoulder while we waited. We didn't talk, but I was glad to be reminded that he was there.

I didn't know how I was going to say good-bye to Andrew.

We waited.

The ambulance crept down the platform and stopped at the far end of the train. People began to get out.

Father patted my shoulder. "Let's go down, Annie." We walked the length of the train toward the men and nurses. Then I saw him. He was talking to a nurse, checking over the list of patients he was escorting.

Andrew. But not Andrew in bathrobe or uniform, the Andrew of the past five months. Now he wore a dark suit, a white shirt and a tie knotted at his collar. His face was all that looked familiar.

He looked up and saw us.

"Morning, Annie. Sir."

I blinked while Father shook his hand. And then Father left to check on the men one last time and I faced Andrew.

"You look different."

He laughed. "Had to buy some clothes to face the world, didn't I?"

"I brought you something." I handed him the package I had been clutching. "It's a book, an atlas of the United States."

"Thank you, Annie. It'll help me find my way. I want to go to a lot of places. Maybe . . . if I can. Maybe even sail up the Nile." He smiled.

I nodded. Behind him, I saw men in wheelchairs and on stretchers being lifted up into the train.

"I have something for you, too." He took a small box out of his pocket and handed it to me. His name was written across the top. Inside lay the Purple Heart.

I looked at him quickly. "You were going to send this home."

"I changed my mind."

"I don't need this anymore for Uncle Paul."

"I know that. But will you keep it for me?"

I touched the smooth black surface of the medal. "Yes," I whispered.

A gust of steam escaped from the train behind me and surrounded us for a moment. Not much time.

"Andrew." My voice still didn't work right and he stepped closer to hear. "About your going." He nodded. I looked down at the cement platform, swallowing to steady my voice. "I said you shouldn't go. But I've been thinking. I wish you weren't, but . . . just don't forget me." I reached out to hold his arm with both my hands. "Come back if you can."

"Thank you, Annie. It'll be easier now." He bent and kissed my cheek.

The conductor slammed the door.

"Andrew, it's time," Father called.

One last squeeze of my hand and Andrew climbed on the train. Then he leaned out the window above my head, waving his bandaged hand. "Good-bye, Annie. I won't forget," he called.

I nodded. I knew he wouldn't forget. Just as I would never forget the moment that I first saw his face.

The train lurched and Andrew grabbed the windowsill, smiling down at me. The train began to move, gradually picking up speed. I stepped back and waved until I couldn't see him anymore. The sun glinted off the last car as I turned toward home.